MERRY EVILMAS

MATT BLISS   L. A. STINNETT   GERRI R. GRAY

CHRISTOPHER BOND   NICOLE WOLVERTON

A. S. MACKENZIE   JOSSLYN DYER

ALAINE GREYSON

ISBN: paperback 978-1-7353926-6-0

Cover Design by Diana TC, triumphcovers.com
Edited by Ashley Olivier

First Printing Edition 2021
Publish by Creative James Media
Pasadena, MD 21122

CONTENTS

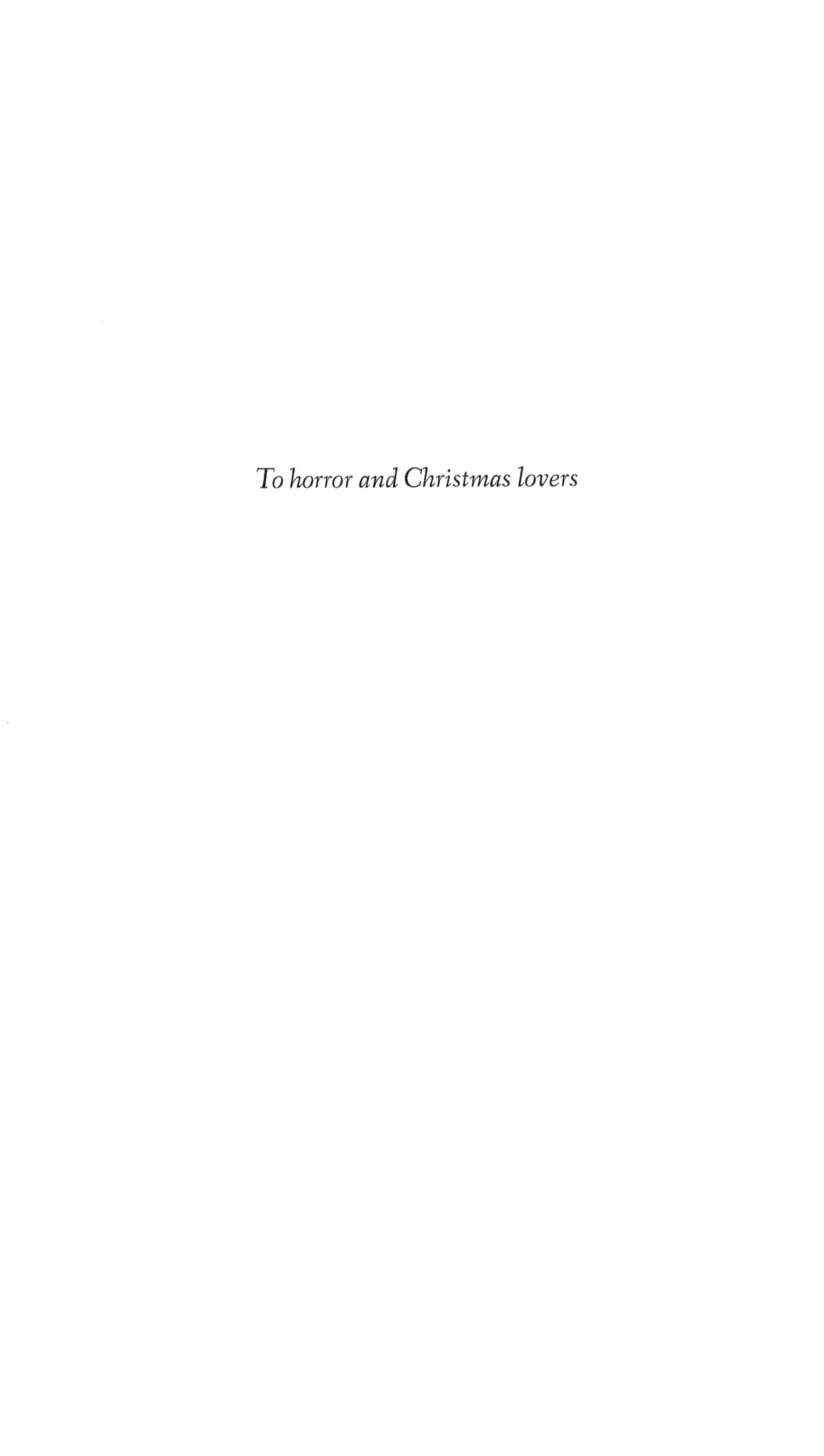

To horror and Christmas lovers

ALL IS MERRY AND BRIGHT
MATT BLISS

Declan stepped outside his bungalow into the cool November air to watch the first snowflakes fall. He surveyed the yard that would soon become his very own *Winter Wonderland*. It was no secret that the quiet mountain town of Brayford Heights started Christmas season early. Each year the local news would air a piece about the "Bright lights in Brayford" and quite often it was Declan's Street that was featured in the shots—never his house, though.

Bundled against the cold, Declan opened the garage door and started pulling red totes down from their shelves. Each one was labeled with the appropriate decorations inside, and each one was laid out in the driveway with meticulous care. Declan spent his entire summer thinking about the theme and painstakingly mapping the layout that included the power demands associated with each outlet.

While busy running extension cords, he noticed his neighbor Nicolas step outside. Even from across the street, Declan could see the man's exaggerated smile. He held up a polite hand to the man, who beamed back before pacing across the street toward him.

"Declan," he said sipping his steaming mug, "you're starting early again, huh? That's just wonderful! Truly, we love it! You always inspire us to add a little more each year. He picked a stray piece of lint off his turtleneck sweater. "Carrie and I are always *so excited* to see what you come up with."

"Thanks, I think this year's going to be good one," Declan replied, brandishing his rolled-up map like a weapon.

"I still can't believe you haven't won yet. Maybe *this* year is going to be *your* year for the trophy, eh?" He sipped his mug and let out a noise of satisfaction. "Oh, where are my manners? Can I get you a cup of hot cocoa? Carrie just made some, and it is to die for —truly!"

"Oh, no thanks, I'm okay. But, yeah, we'll see if it is *my* year for the trophy. I mean, I'll have to beat you first to get it." Declan let out an awkward laugh.

"Hey that's the spirit! Isn't that what this is all about, though?" Nicholas said with his chin raised to the flurry of falling flakes. "The spirit of Christmas!"

"Right ..." Declan squinted at the man before turning back to his work.

"So, did you hear Maria is going to be one of the judges this year.

Declan's heart flickered at the mention of her name. "You don't say ..."

"Yeah, what better way to introduce her to the neighborhood than to give her the clipboard? A perfect, impartial judge if I must say so."

"Yes," Declan agreed, "*perfect!*"

"Well, I better get back to Carrie. Don't be afraid to holler if you need a hand. After all, what are neighbors for?"

"Right." Declan smiled. "What *are* neighbors for?"

He turned back to his work while visions of multi-colored lights blinked on in his head.

December came with its usual its blankets of snow that somehow glittered under the blue Brayford Heights sky. Snowmen in black hats and plaid scarves stood posted outside the picturesque homes while their owners went to work hanging festive lights and decorations.

While most were only beginning this joyous Brayford tradition, a few residents were already well along their way with hopes of winning the coveted "Best Overall" trophy in the town contest.

Declan spent night and day in the cold to create the light display that might finally win him the competition, but from the looks of it, Nicholas was apt to win again. Somehow, the home across from him was lit up with glowing candy canes, lighted trees, toy soldiers, nutcrackers, and all eight of Santa's reindeers, plus

Rudolph—all blazing bright in their power consuming glory. What Declan found odd, was that he had yet to see Nicolas—or anyone, for that matter—outside putting any of it up.

Declan squinted at the yard from the top of his ladder, trying to finally catch someone in the act, when he heard a soft voice below.

"Wow, Declan! This is looking amazing!"

He looked over his shoulder and almost fell off the ladder when he saw who it was. Maria's brown curls spilled out from under her knit hat and hung over her small shoulders.

"You think so?" Declan asked as he stepped down the ladder, flashing a smile in return. He sucked in the gut that his forty-five-year-old metabolism refused to get rid of while watching Maria's eyes sparkle in the lights surrounding them.

"Absolutely!" she replied. "I can't believe I have to judge all these wonderful homes. I am completely out of my element, by the way."

"Don't worry, I'm sure you're going to fit right in," Declan said while trying not to think of her lips. "Are you adjusting to the weather? Pretty far from what you were used to in L.A. I bet."

"You know, I'm starting to get used to it. Yeah, it's cold, but who could complain about getting to live in a Christmas card?" She wrapped her arms around herself to hold in the warmth while looking over the twinkling lights of Declan's yard.

"This truly is amazing, Declan!" Her smile was far from the stuck-up divorcee that some of the others made her out to be.

Declan was overwhelmed with pride. So much so, he tried something very uncharacteristic of himself. "So, Maria." He paused as her brown eyes locked onto his. "I was thinking that ... if you ever wanted to—"

"Maria! Declan! Stay there and let me grab my coat." Nicholas waved from his porch with a smile whiter than the surrounding snow.

Declan instantly deflated. There were only a few times in his life where he mustered up the courage to ask out a pretty girl—and Nicholas just screwed up one of them.

"Boy, this is such a magical time of year, isn't it?" Nicholas said to the two of them as he approached.

"Right ... magical," Declan said through gritted teeth.

"Hi, Nick. I see you're about ready for the contest too, huh?" Maria gestured to his monstrosity of lights.

"You know, I don't even think about the contest anymore. For me, it's about the spirt of the season." He looked up and away while he talked. Declan *hated* how he did this.

"Well ... I should get going, but it was good seeing you, Nick! And thanks for talking to me, Declan. I'll see you round." Maria flashed a smile at Declan before climbing into her car and leaving.

"Boy, she sure is something, eh, bud?" Nicholas turned and placed an arm around Declan's shoulders. "Such a shame, though, having to spend Christmas alone.

I don't know what I would do without Carrie. I really am a blessed man!"

"Nick," Declan replied while cringing out of his neighbors embrace, "I'm going to get back to what I was doing." He motioned towards the rows of golden lights covering his yard.

"Oh, right! I'll leave you to it, but remember if you—"

"Need a hand; yeah, I got it Nick, but thanks anyways ..."

Nicholas had only taken three steps back to his house before his foot crunched down on a golden bulb, smashing it with a *pop*. The entire run of lights across Declan's yard went dark. Nicholas turned to Declan with his mouth twisted up in a tooth-filled grin.

Declan glared in disbelief. *The prick meant to do that!*

In Declan's mind, *this* had crossed the line! As if losing to a man—*this man*— who was never even seen putting up lights each year wasn't bad enough, he robbed Declan of a chance at love, and now he had destroyed his precious lights. Declan's thoughts turned redder than Santa's sleigh.

He stalked across the lawn, and snatched up the red and white-striped handle of the snow shovel with 'Let it Snow' painted on its face. He reared it back and with one thunderous blow, Declan brought it down into the back of Nicholas's head. The shovel rang out like a church bell on Christmas morning, and the man dropped like a sack of coal to the frozen street below. Declan raised the shovel above his head and brought it down a second time. *The bell sounded again.*

Nicolas's head *popped* like a chestnut on an open fire; blood and brain matter spilled to the icy street. Declan stepped back to avoid getting the cranberry sauce spilling from Nicholas's split skull on his boots. He knew from one look at him that the man was dead.

A cold surge of panic gripped him. He whipped his head round, looking for anyone watching. *Looking for witnesses.* He grabbed hold of Nicholas's wellingtons, and started sliding him across the ice. It was as if he was outside his body, watching as a man who looked just like him, dragged the lifeless corpse of his neighbor in a trail of blood.

Declan spotted the 'Santa's Workshop' decoration surrounded with plastic candy canes in his yard. It was actually a doghouse he had painted to resemble the tiny elves workshop, but it was *just* big enough to hide a body. Declan opened the small door and heaved Nicolas inside. After some quick handiwork with the same snow shovel used to kill the man, the street looked like its normal, jolly self again.

Declan's heart worked faster than Santa's elves when he returned home. He was horrified by what he'd done, but there was no going back. He killed a man and stuffed the body inside his Christmas decorations. He paced the length of his large bay window while sneaking glances at the tiny house.

What-do-I-do? What-do-I-do? What-do-I-do?

Declan was worried. Worried about losing the contest, yes, but most of all, worried about losing *the girl*. He considered his options while his feet traced lines in the carpet.

Only two days until the contest. Without Nicholas, that trophy might finally be mine! I'll get the trophy, get the girl, and then I'll confess to what I did. I just need this one perfect day first!

The next morning, Declan was whistling a Christmas tune while fixing the bulb his neighbor broke the previous day. He was careful to make sure each and every bulb was burning bright enough for his satisfaction. He worked like a man who knew there was *nothing* to stop him.

While dragging the red overstuffed chair he planned to sit in while dressed as Santa for the judging, Maria came out her house next door and spotted the man at work.

"Still at it, Declan?" she said with a smile warmer than cinnamon. She was still in her pajamas and slippers.

He nodded. "Where else is Santa going to sit when he comes?"

"Oh, well *if* he comes, you let me know. I still have to tell him what I want this year." She raised an eyebrow at Declan.

"Whatcha gonna ask for?"

"I'm not tellin' you! Are *you* Santa?"

"You never know ... I might be. I mean ... I *could* be!"

She laughed, waving him off and reached for the paper at her doorstep. "Hey," she said, gesturing the paper toward Nicolas's house, "I see our friend has been hard at work too."

Declan froze. This didn't seem possible since Nicholas was dead in his painted doghouse. He turned to see that more decorations *did* in fact get added across the street. A twelve-foot inflatable Santa stood fixed to the garage roof along with several more strings of lights.

"Should I go tell that Santa instead?" Maria asked.

Declan didn't hear her. The sight of the massive Santa Clause left him paralyzed with fear.

How the fuck is this possible? His eyes kept flicking back to the tiny workshop.

"Declan? You okay?" Maria shouted.

"What?" He snapped his head back toward her.

"I asked if you're okay. I lost you for a minute there." Her large brown eyes suddenly looked concerned.

"Yeah, I was uh ... just thinking, I guess."

She shook her brown curls. "Don't stay out too long. You'll freeze to death out here," she replied with a polite smile before walking back inside.

The moment her door shut, Declan crunched through the snow as fast he could. He flung open the small door to see Nicholas's frozen corpse staring back at him with Icicles hanging from the dead man's contorted face.

He turned in disbelief and faced the glowing house. *It looked better than his did.* Declan couldn't figure out who had put up the decorations—or when—but he *did* know that he had to do more or else he'd never win.

❄

Declan stayed out until the sun went down. He added lighted icicles, wrote 'NOEL' on the side of his house in lights, and almost doubled the amount of decorations he had in the yard. Once satisfied that his house would be declared the victor, he headed in to warm himself by the fire. This time, he knew that the trophy would be his.

The microwave single serving meal was still frozen in the center when Declan sat down alone at his table. He poked the gelatinous sauce while his thoughts kept going back the frozen body in 'Santa's Workshop' and the lights that were mysteriously multiplying across the street.

It was possible, he considered, that Nicholas's wife did it, but Declan was outside night and day and had yet to see a single person on the property. Twice during his meal, Declan went to the window to watch the workshop.

His thoughts dashed from one outlandish possibility to the next before each time landing on Maria. He could still see her big brown eyes all aglow from the glittering lights around them. He thought about those same brown eyes gleaming when she'd hand *him* the trophy before being swept away in a passionate kiss under the mistletoe.

The thought made Declan feel bolder than ever. Surely, he decided, no one could stop him now, so he pushed aside the lukewarm food and reached for the phone.

Maria picked up after the second ring, "Hello?"

"Uh ... hi Maria, it's Declan. Sorry for calling so late ..."

"Hey, Declan," she stretched his name out. He could practically hear her *twirling* her hair. "It's okay; I was just watching some cheesy Christmas movie. So, what's up?"

He paced his living room with the phone pressed to his ear.

"So, I was eating dinner, and thought about how nice I

might be if ... some night ... maybe you and I could eat dinner? Together, I mean."

His eyes glanced out the window to 'Santa's Workshop'.

"Are you asking me out on a date?"

"Yeah," he said with a boldness, "actually, I am! I would love to ..."

His words trailed off as he saw movement at Nicholas's house. He jolted to the window and pressed his face to the glass. A dark shape moved across the top of Nicholas's house, laying a trail of bright lights behind it.

"How about after the contest judging, tomorrow? We can go out to celebrate?"

He was only half listening. Declan's eyes focused on the figure across the street. Even through the darkness, it looked far too large for him to make sense of it.

"Uh ... yeah, that would be great ..."

He squinted hard. The dark figure stopped and turned toward Declan, waving a shadowed hand.

"It's a date!" Maria said. "I'll see you tomorrow, and don't forget your Santa suit!"

"Right ... Santa suit ..." Declan hung up the phone and ran outside.

From his porch, Declan could see the figure move across the roof in quick, herky-jerky movements. Its dark limbs spanned the width of his roof as they placed row after row of glowing bulbs. He watched in terror as the lights spelled out words.

Ho-Ho-Ho ... The fucker is spelling Ho-Ho-Ho!

It stopped in the bulbs' golden glow and turned to Declan. Bulbous eyes burned red as if they had lights of their own. It pulled its skin back into a harrowing smile. One big enough to split its massive head in half and reveal rows of long skinny teeth hanging down like yellowed icicles.

Its mouth clamped shut before it disappeared over the side of the roof. Declan ran across the street, sliding across the ice in his house slippers, but the creature was gone. He froze, looking over what the creature left behind.

It looks fucking amazing! Shit!

Declan went inside and put on a proper coat and boots before leaving for the hardware store. He had a long night ahead of him if he was going to keep up.

It was almost noon before Declan finally managed to pull himself out of bed. He worked through the night installing the sound system, snowflake projectors, and the twelve-foot-long mural made of lights with Santa and his reindeer eating dinner in a mockup of *The Last Supper*. Despite only a few hours' sleep, Declan felt invigorated. This was because it was finally the day of the judging.

After pouring a fresh cup of coffee, Declan moved to his front window and breathed a sigh of relief when he couldn't spot any new decorations at Nicholas's house. His eyes flicked to the painted doghouse that held his neighbors corpse and was taken back by the small crowd of children gathered round his yard.

"Must be admiring the decorations," he murmured while watching them with a smile. There was nothing as wondrous as seeing *his* display spark joy in a child's eyes. The children laughed and smiled as one climbed up on the lap of the Santa sitting in the oversize chair he set outside. Fear struck Declan like a cold snowball to the face at the realization that *he didn't put anything in the chair.*

Declan dropped his coffee and stormed out the house in his robe. Sitting in the plush chair was Nicholas's frozen corpse dressed in a jolly red suite and long silver beard. A small girl sat in its lap, reaching toward its beard as the other children laughed.

Declan plowed through the snow, "HEY! GET OUT OF HERE!" he yelled, trying to shoo them away. "GET OFF OF HIM!"

The other kids backed away, scared and bewildered, but the little girl shriveled in its lap, too frightened to move. Declan, robe half-undone, ran right at her with his face twisted in wild anger.

"WHAT THE HELL ARE YOU DOING? GET OFF OF HIM!"

The small girl screamed and burst into tears. Declan reached toward her as his eyes bulged from his head until Maria's voice stopped him. She ran between the two and helped the small girl down.

"What the hell is wrong with you, Declan?" she asked as she held the small girl. "She's just a kid, and it's just a *dumb* decoration!" She gave him a shame filled stare as she walked the crying girl away.

He stood in the winter chill until feeling a cold wetness seep into his slippers and turned back to the dressed body on his lawn. He snuck a look to the dead man's house and stopped on the dark creature in the yard across from him. Its red snow-globe eyes focused on him with its mouth pulled back in the same oversized smile. Its sinewy body convulsed in a raspy laugh.

Declan grabbed a plastic candy cane and threw it towards the thing while shouting, "You son-of-a-bitch! I'll kill you for this!" It turned and scrambled up the side of the house with long, smooth strides like that of a spider before disappearing behind the roof.

Declan muscled Nicholas's frozen remains back into the workshop before putting on winter clothes. Not only was this freakish creature destroying his chances of winning the contest, but now he looked like a maniac in front of Maria. He all but assumed the date was off after the awful look in her eyes. All he had left now, was the contest.

He grabbed the snow shovel and stormed across the street. "Come on out here, you asshole!" he shouted to his murdered neighbor's roof. "I'm gonna find you! And when I do ..." He swung the snow shovel into one of the plastic toy soldiers, destroying it in an explosion of colored plastic.

He destroyed three more nutcrackers and leaned on his shovel to catch his breath. That's when he heard the *pop*, and *crinkle* of shattered glass. This sound wasn't from his shovel, but from *his* side of the street. Declan spun in time to see the dark creature smiling at him from *his* roof where he pointed a long black claw at one of the many bulbs lining the house. It paused only a moment before smashing the bulb in its hand, flashing its teeth.

"No!" Declan yelled as he ran back. The creature shuddered with laughter through its large, horrid teeth. Its mouth unhinged wide enough to swallow a reindeer whole. Declan circled his house with madness in his eyes. He shouted taunts to his roof while swinging the snow shovel madly.

When he finally leaned the ladder against the house and climbed up to the top, the creature was gone.

Declan worked at repairing what the creature destroyed and had just finished replacing the last bulb when a group of warm, puffy jackets holding clipboards moved their way down the street.

The judges lined up outside Nicholas's house while speaking in hushed tones and scribbling on clipboards, but Declan kept his eyes fixed on one of them. He felt sick when he watched Maria smile and nod to one of the other judges, pointing to the flashing 'North Pole' display.

After an excruciating ten minutes, the judges finally turned in his direction. A surge of excitement large enough to blow a fuse ran through Declan when Saw Maria smile at him.

This is what I've been waiting for! This is my year!

He once again saw the trophy in his hands as Maria moved in for her kiss. The judges had just formed their firing line, when Declan shouted, "It's my turn now!" and pressed play on his control board. He waited for the Christmas music. He waited for the dancing snowflakes. But all at once, instead of the grand performance, his house went dark—the power died.

He pressed the button repeatedly, pushing harder each time but instead of his *Winter Wonderland* coming back to life, only the high-pitched laugh of the creature was heard. Feeling the familiar rage surge through him, Declan grabbed the snow shovel, and followed the noise.

He rounded the corner ready to kill the beast once and for all, just as he did Nicholas. But when he turned in the narrow alleyway, and saw the long black nails slice through the power meter in a burst of sparks, his rage turned to something else: fear.

The tall black creature looked down on Declan before taking one sweeping step toward him. Its large black head split almost in half as it let out another laugh and raised a leathered hand toward him.

Declan swing the shovel at the creature, hoping to hear that same church bell gong, but the massive hand caught it, plucking it away like it was a toothpick in an *hors d'œuvres*. It brought the shovel to its mouth before snapping it shut like a bear trap, chewing though metal and wood with ease.

At the sight of this, Declan ran. He moved through the maze of dark decorations, *his decorations*, while hearing snow crunch under heavy footsteps behind him. He heard its raspy laughter—he heard it clicking its teeth—but what scared him the most was what he heard from the crowd in the street.

"...and it should come as no surprise, the winner once again is Nicholas!"

The crowd clapped until Declan ran at them. "Wait! That's impossible!" Declan charged into the group, suddenly forgetting what was chasing him. "HE'S DEAD! I KILLED HIM! He can't win if he's *dead!*"

The crowd fell silent as all eyes turned to him, including Maria's.

"Come look! He's dead inside my damn dog-house!"

Declan went to the small house and opened the door. *Nicholas was gone.*

"Wait ... that can't be! I killed him! I bashed his head in with a shovel and ..."

The group stared at Declan with lowered brows, pressing closer to the panicked man.

"It was the damn monster! He hid the body! I know it! He can't win! He's dead! That's my trophy! IT'S MINE!"

Declan looked into the angry faces of his neighbors surrounding him, now only paces away.

"I'M THE WINNER! ME!"

Someone in the crowd said, "Get him!" and they charged with reaching hands and exposed teeth. Declan turned to run, but the towering black creature stopped him. It smiled before its jaw unhinged, revealing its long, yellowed teeth. Declan looked into his massive mouth and screamed as it shoved him inside, and his world went dark.

"**D**eclan ...*Can you hear me?*"
Declan opened his eyes to see the clear blue sky above with the many faces of his neighbors staring at him.

"There you are ... are you okay? The ambulance is here, okay? Just focus on me ..."

Declan looked up into Nicholas's face, still holding that gleaming white smile.

"Wha ... what happened? I thought you were dead?" said Declan as he tried to sit up.

"Dead? No, no. You fell off your roof putting up Christmas lights. We thought you were a goner for a minute there!"

Declan blinked until the picture came into view. He was laying on a pile of rubble that used to be 'Santa's Workshop' with a leg bent back at an odd angle.

"No, no ... I ... I killed you, Nick! I bashed your head in with a shovel! Your brains splattered on the street! The damn monster!"

Nicholas lost his award-winning smile. "Declan, you're not making any sense! Just hang on, okay?" Nicholas waved to the paramedics pushing a gurney through the snow.

Declan screamed as they loaded him onto the stretcher, "I was going to win! I killed you, Nick! I would have won, but that *fucking* monster!"

Declan watched Nicholas as they loaded him onto the stretcher. He watched his neighbor put an arm around Maria and kiss her head. "Don't worry, Carrie. He's going to be fine ..."

"She was mine, you son-of-a-bitch! It was all supposed to be MINE!"

They pushed him into the ambulance with a clatter of metal and greased bearings, and Nicholas stepped inside after.

"Declan," he said, pulling a stray piece of lint from his sweater, "if you need a hand, let me know. *That's* what neighbors are for after all." Nicholas moved close, placing his face close to Declan's, "but if you try to fuck me over again," his face grew dark and his mouth unhinged, exposing pointed yellowed teeth, "you won't be so lucky next time!"

Declan screamed as Nicholas climbed from the ambulance and flung the door shut. The sirens blared to life with lights flashing a brilliant blue and red until turning the corner and disappearing from sight. Nicholas placed an arm around his wife. "It's sad," he said as he turned his chin up and away, "some people have to spend their Christmas alone. I don't know what I would do without you." He smiled a toothy grin that seemed to split his head in two.

"I really am a blessed man!"

LAST CHRISTMAS
CHRISTOPHER BOND

The windows of the quaint brick house glowed warmly against the night sky. It was just one of perhaps a dozen houses on the narrow street where the sounds of talk and laughter and the singing of Christmas carols drifted out to mingle with the slowly falling snowflakes that coated everything like a fine layer of crushed opal. The entire neighborhood sparkled like a thousand glittery ornaments. Strings of red and green lights strewn along the house's gables flashed merrily in time with the cheerful music coming from within. On the front steps, the lights reflected off of the old man's worried face. Shannon was about to ring the doorbell when she noticed.

"Are you alright, Martin? Is something wrong?"

The man looked down at his feet. His worn leather boots were falling apart, mostly held together by force of will than by merit of their construction. At least his rumpled army jacket and stained sweatpants seemed to match the tattered Santa hat perched upon his long, greasy hair. It had been a long time since Martin Ridley had worried about such things. In fact, it had been a long time since he'd worried about anything besides finding a hot meal or a dry place to sleep.

Something *was* wrong, of course. *Everything* was wrong.

Shannon saw a timid frown hiding beneath his wiry beard. She stepped away from the door and put an arm around the man's shoulder. "They're good people, you know? They're my family." she said. "They won't bite, I promise."

Martin looked up and gave Shannon a sheepish smile. A thin stream of tears trickled down his dirty, wrinkled cheeks. "You–you don't have to do this, you know," he said, his voice a paper-thin sigh. "I appreciate the gesture, I really do, but–the holidays are for being with family, and well– you should be able to spend it with yours without having to put up with some stranger. Maybe you could just bring a plate of food out to me or something." He looked to the stone steps again. "I'm afraid I'm not the best company these days...or the cleanest."

"Nonsense!" Shannon tittered. "They'll be so happy to have you."

It had been nearly three months since she'd been home from college, almost a year since she'd seen most of her extended family that was gathered inside her parents' home. She'd noticed Martin outside of the bus station, shivering under a thin flannel blanket, his breath whooshing out in great frozen clouds. She'd almost walked past him with hardly a second thought, but then the old man had leaned out and wished her a Merry Christmas. He reached into his coat, and for a second, Shannon felt a pang of fear. But when he pulled his hand back out, he was holding a tiny silver bell. He shook it once, then handed it to her and smiled. Something about the way he looked at her pulled on faint memories from her childhood, of visiting Santa Claus at the mall and asking for presents, of leaving cookies and milk and carrots for the reindeer by the fireplace. It reminded her of when Christmas was more than just parties and drinking and gift cards between friends. It reminded her of when Christmas was *magic*. *We can all use a little more magic*, she thought. *The world is tough all over.*

She patted the old man on the back and turned to the door. "You'll be great company, Martin, I'm sure of it. And if Uncle Terry is as drunk as I *think* he'll be, then you won't have to worry about saying too much anyway. He'll do enough talking for all of us!" She pressed doorbell, and the first few bars of "Come All Ye Faithful" chimed from somewhere inside the house.

The door opened, and the sounds of laughter and song spilled into the night, buffeted by the smells of cinnamon and pine and oaken logs burning in the fireplace. A balding, middle-aged man in a gaudy turtleneck smiled out from behind his round eyeglasses, his face as warm as a batch of freshly baked sugar cookies.

"Shannon!" the man cried, grinning. "Come in, come in! We've all been waiting for you to get here!"

Shannon walked inside and squeezed the man with a laugh. She took off her stocking hat and unzipped her insulated vest. "Uncle Terry! I was *just* telling my friend about you." She nodded back towards the steps where Martin was standing. "Uncle Terry, this is my friend, Martin. We met at the bus station...I asked him if he'd like to come over and celebrate with us this year."

Uncle Terry peered out and noticed Martin standing there for the first time. His smile faltered, but to his credit he had it back in place in just a moment. "Uh, hi there,

Martin!" Uncle Terry reached a hand across the threshold. "Terry Peters. It's nice to meet you."

Martin took Uncle Terry's hand and shook it. His face shone red with embarrassment, but he didn't look away from the man's smiling eyes. "I'm–I'm pleased to meet you too, Terry. Your niece is a very kind person. I hope I'm not intruding."

"No, not at all." He shook a glass tumbler filled with ice and a yellow-brown liquid. "We have a whole bowl of rum and eggnog, and unless somebody starts helping me get rid of it, I think Pam is going to be mighty upset with me tomorrow."

They all laughed, and Terry and Shannon started into the house. They had just reached the staircase before Shannon realized that Martin hadn't followed them in. Terry wandered into the living room, and Shannon walked back to the front door. The old man was still standing on the stoop.

"Hey, are you having second thoughts?" she asked.

Martin looked down, but only briefly. "No, it's just–I haven't been invited inside." He shuffled awkwardly. "I'm a bit old-fashioned, I suppose."

"Well, come in already!" Shannon laughed. She reached out and took his hand, pulling him into the foyer, and Martin smiled the first genuine smile she'd seen all night.

Martin looked around the foyer in wonder, like a child who had just walked into the world's largest toy store. Long stands of garland were coiled around a gleaming wooden banister, and from the garland hung a string of red Santa hats like festive pennants. A large wreath hung from the backside of the front door, and tiny crystal angels smiled and sang carols among clusters of red and silver bells woven between the branches.

Shannon looked at the way Martin's eyes were shining, and warmth bubbled up from deep inside of her, somewhere down in her heart, and it spread slowly through her body. It was the Christmas magic; her body tingled with it. She was glad she'd brought him. She'd made the right choice.

Martin walked around the foyer, taking it all in. He ran a finger along the garland and felt the end of one fuzzy hat. He turned to the giant wreath and flicked one of the tiny bells. It chirped cheerily, and the old man's face broke into a hundred wrinkles. He surprised himself when a hoarse, barking laugh came coughing out from under his breath like an old engine sputtering into life after a decade of disuse. He looked at Shannon with eyes wide with amazement, and they both broke into a fit of laughter like old friends who had passed a familiar inside joke. Martin dabbed the corner of his eye with a sleeve, and then he froze, his smile wilting on his face. Laughter burst from the next room, and Martin stepped backwards, a hand held up in front of him. His legs wobbled, and Shannon thought the poor man might collapse.

She rushed to his side. "Whoa! Are you okay?" She braced her hands to steady him. The laughter roared again like a volley of gunfire, and then she understood. She patted Martin on his back. "I get it," she said, nodding slowly. "You're nervous about meeting everyone."

Martin gazed back across the room to where he had been standing. There was a Christmas clock on the wall, one with Santa's sleigh on one hand and Rudolph on the other, and it was hung next to a shelf where a few dozen glimmering handbells were displayed. Below the shelf, a ceramic nativity scene had been set up on a side table, Mary and Joseph and the Wise Men surrounded by a menagerie of farm animals. In the center, the baby Jesus lay swaddled in his filthy wooden manger. The infant Savior. The old man shuddered. He looked back to Shannon and nodded. The color had drained from his face. He forced a weak smile.

"Yeah. Yeah, I guess I am." He gestured around the room. There was pain etched onto his kind features, sorrow drooping from every wrinkle. "This place it–it's lovely. But it reminds me a lot of other holidays. I have a lot of bad memories tied around Noel. The ghosts of Christmas's past, I suppose." He cleared his throat. "I guess I've been alone for too long."

"I'm sorry, Martin. I'm sorry to hear that." It broke her heart a little–and made her feel a little guilty–to think that such a joyous time of the year for her could bring such sorrow to others. Shannon leaned in and hugged him. He flinched, his body tense and rigid; it was like embracing an ironing board. "I take it you don't have much family around here?" she asked him.

"No, I think I'm the only one left. It feels like it's been a hundred years since I've had anyone."

"Well, that's okay, Martin. Tonight, you'll have a whole house full of family. Tonight, you'll be one of us."

"Thank you, Shannon. Sincerely. I already feel like I'm surrounded by friends."

When they walked into the living room, everyone turned, and a chorus of cheers erupted. Two muscled teenage boys with crewcuts were sitting on the couch looking like a pair of linebackers, their phones glued to their meaty hands. Uncle Terry was standing near the Christmas tree next to a tall woman with long, brown hair, and beside them another middle-aged couple stood with their own Santa hats on, drinks in hand.

An elderly woman in a cardigan tottered over to Shannon, her glasses hanging from a lanyard around her neck, her arms outstretched. "Shannon," she cried. "My baby girl, how I've missed you." Shannon bent down, and the woman wrapped her arms around her. "Grandma!" Shannon cooed. "Oh, the house smells lovely. Nobody cooks like you at the university." The old woman cackled. "Of course not, dear, I could have told you that! But I can't take credit; your sister is in there whipping up quite the spread. Are you hungry?"

"Starving."

"Good." Grandma looked over to Martin, who had been hanging back slightly. "And who is this, dear?"

"This is my friend, Martin." The rumble of conversation stopped. A log popped in the fireplace. Grandma stared at the man in the worn army jacket and the lopsided Santa hat.

"Well," she said, "we all thought you might show up with a boy from school, but I suppose *he's* handsome enough in a pinch."

"Grandma!" Shannon gasped, and everyone broke into laughter. Even Martin couldn't help himself. The old woman walked over to Martin and took his hand. "Martin, I'm Marie. *Grandma* Marie if you want to make a woman feel old. We're so happy you'll be joining us." Martin stammered out a hurried thank you. Grandma nodded. "You'll want to be careful, though, young man," she intoned. "You're standing under the mistletoe." She nodded up above the doorway where a tiny bouquet of green branches and red berries were tied. He chuckled softly. She was a well-kept woman, he noticed. Her skin was flushed and smooth, and her eyes danced with youthful exuberance. "Oh, I think it's *you* who best be careful, Marie," he said, and everyone laughed again, and the party continued.

The others came up in small groups and introduced themselves. The tall woman with the brown hair was Aunt Pam. Martin would have known that without introduction, of course, the way the woman frowned at Uncle Terry's quickly diminishing glasses of spiked eggnog. The other middle-aged couple were David and Janet, Shannon's parents. David handed Martin a drink and shook his hand. "Nice to meet you, Martin," he said, only slightly slurring from the booze. "A merry Christmas to you! And I love the hat, by the way."

Janet echoed his sentiments, adding, "Shannon's a great judge of character, you know. I was hoping she'd bring someone over. It gets so *boring* with the same old crowd." She winked and laughed. The two muscle-bound teenagers were Will and Tommy, Terry and Pam's twin sons. They looked away from their phones for almost a full minute to grunt their greetings before sitting back down on the couch.

"So," Uncle Terry began, "where are you from, Martin?" Shannon was talking with her cousins on the couch, and the older adults had gathered over by the brightly lit tree in the corner. Martin had been a ball of nerves upon first entering the house, his insides like a mass of tangled wire, but the rum had relaxed him. It helped that Terry and David made sure his glass was never empty.

"Oh, from all over, really." He took a sip from his drink. "My father had a job that kept him moving, and my mother and I moved with him, dragged along behind with all of our belongings in suitcases and knapsacks."

"Was he in the army or something?" Aunt Pam asked.

"No," Martin said. "He was a drunk."

David snorted, his hand moving much too slowly towards his mouth to stifle it, and Janet shot him a cool glance. Martin held out his hands. "No, no, please" he said, laughing a bit himself. "It's okay to laugh. It wasn't very funny then, but that was a long time ago. I really shouldn't disparage him like that anyway, he loved us dearly." Martin smiled, but it was a sad smile. His eyes were far away.

The others shot each other a glance, unsure of what to say. Martin didn't notice. His eyes refocused, and he said, "He was a good man. Or he tried to be." He lifted his glass. "To my father. And to everyone that can't be with us any longer. You were loved, and you are missed." The others nodded. They clinked their glasses together and drank.

Uncle Terry stepped away. He shook his empty glass. "Looks like my drink's broken. Guess I'd better head into the kitchen and fix it. Anyone else need a refill?"

"I'll help you," Martin said.

"No, that's okay. You're a guest here."

"I insist. You only have two arms, and I see at least five empty glasses."

S hannon looked around the room with tense awareness. The tingling she'd felt earlier in the night–the feeling she'd mistaken for that old Christmas magic–had solidified into a hot, leaden ball of dread in the pit of her stomach. Something wasn't right. The others felt it too; she could tell by the way they milled about, sipping at their drinks halfheartedly, casting furtive glances to the clock on the mantle. Where was Martin? And where was Uncle Terry? She checked her phone. *It's almost time to eat. They should be back by now. What's taking them so long?* She sat up quickly. Alarm bells were ringing in her head, louder even than Burl Ives who was currently pleading from beyond the grave for everyone to have a holly jolly Christmas.

Shannon brushed past her parents and stalked out of the living room and through the kitchen doorway.

"What's gotten into her?" David asked Janet. "Too much eggnog?"

"School can be a stressful time, David. Don't be too harsh on her." He nodded and took another sip of his drink.

A terrible scream tore through the house, and David's glass tumbled from his hand and crashed onto the carpet. It was Shannon's scream, and it was coming from the kitchen. There was a pause, just an instant, when everyone looked to each other in bewilderment, eyes wide and questioning. Even Burl Ives seemed to stop and catch his breath for a moment.

Then everyone ran towards the kitchen and the source of the screaming.

David and Janet got there first. The screams had broken up into a flurry of angry, shrieking cries, harsh words thrown like so many poison-tipped spears.

Shannon was standing on one side of the kitchen island, a butcher knife held in front of her with a shaking hand. She was screaming like a banshee. Screaming at Martin.

Martin was covered in blood. His face and his beard were all but dripping with it. He held Uncle Terry in one arm, cradling the chubby man like you would a drunken friend stumbling home from the bar. Martin's other hand was wrapped around the end of a hefty wooden stake, the other end of it sunk up to his fist into Terry's chest. Violently red blood spurted from the wound and cascaded over Martin's face. The old man stared at everyone, with eyes bright and smoldering. He looked back to Shannon and gave the spike another wrenching twist, driving it in even further. Blood poured hot and thick like cranberry sauce out of the gaping wound and down onto the tiled floor.

"What the *fuck*, Martin!" Shannon spat at him, her face wet with tears. "What the *fuck* is wrong with you, you crazy asshole! Jesus Christ!"

"Let him go!" Aunt Pam said. "Please, god, let him go! He's losing a lot of blood!"

"Let's get the bastard!" Tommy screamed, grabbing a long carving knife from the counter. Will was right behind his brother, his clenched fists held out like miniature bulldozers. "You mangy prick!" he screamed. "You're ours now!" The family all crowded together and advanced on the old man.

"Stay back!" Martin hissed. He let go of the stake and reached into his grimy army coat, grabbing for something. When he found it, he pulled it out and thrust it into the space between him and the encroaching family. "By the power of God, stay back, you monsters!" he screamed.

In his outstretched hand, he held a large silver crucifix, the metal inlaid with bits of amethyst and swirling gold filigree. An iron Christ was pinned to the cross, his arms wide, his face pinched in agony. Martin waved it at them like a loaded pistol, and they flinched and faltered, stopping dead in their tracks. Martin's breathing was heavy and ragged, but the look on his face was pure triumph. He let go of Terry's body, and it slumped to the floor with a sickening splash.

"I know who you are," he gasped out. "Better, I know

what you are." His heart was thundering like a stampede of wild horses, and it rattled his thin frame and his frail, papery lungs, but his voice stayed strong and steady. "I've been watching you for a very long time. All of you!" He nodded towards Shannon. "Especially *you*." The ghost of a smile lifted the corners of his mouth. "The most likely to show an old man a bit of hospitality during a cold, winter night. Or maybe you were just hungry, out on the prowl for a nice Christmastide feast." He chuckled mirthlessly. "I knew you'd be my way in. And I thank you."

"Fuck you!" Shannon screamed. "You're deranged! Too many drugs or too much booze. Probably both."

"Deranged, huh? That's rich. Especially coming from one of *you*." Martin countered. "If I'm deranged, then what's *this*?" He dug in his pocket and lifted out a golden-glazed handbell, one of the ones that had been displayed on the shelf behind the nativity set in the foyer. It caught the kitchen lights and twinkled like the Star of Bethlehem.

Shannon looked at it incredulously. "I, uh," she stammered. She looked to her dad and her mom, to her aunt and her grandma and her cousins, but they were all silent, as stunned as her. "That's just a–a decoration. A stupid Christmas trinket. It's meaningless." Her face grew hot with anger. Her voice wavered. "You killed my uncle for *that*?" A moment of doubt passed over the old man's face, and the cross lowered slightly. Shannon continued, her voice gaining momentum like a hell-bound train just leaving the station. Tommy inched forward around the edge of the island. "You murdered him for a useless *bell*?" Shannon ranted. Spittle flew from between her crimson lips. "Why not just rob us then, if that's what you intended all along? Why'd you have to kill him? Why'd you have to kill my uncle?"

Tommy took another step, but it was a bit too big, and Martin raised the cross again. The boy stopped. Martin coughed out a bitter laugh.

"Very convincing, Shannon. Almost had me there for a second. Now, if you'll kindly *shut the fuck up*, we can get on with this." Her face went white, then red again, her lips pulled back into a snarl. They were all snarling. "Ah, that's better, isn't it?" Martin continued. "It's so tiresome to wear a mask all of the time." He shook the handbell, and it rang merrily in the silence of the kitchen. "This isn't just any useless trinket. I'm sure you all know that, though. Those bells out there, the ones you display so proudly—so *cruelly*—those aren't yours. They belonged to good men and women who got caught up in bad situations, people trying to better their lives by helping others. Some of them were my friends. But this one–*this* belonged to my father. He took it with him on the last night my mom and I ever saw him. On the night he disappeared. That was almost forty years ago."

He looked ruefully down to the prone, bleeding form of Uncle Terry, and then back up to the rest of those in the room.

"My dad was an alcoholic and an addict, and he made shit-poor decisions. But deep down, he wanted to be a good man. He *tried* to be a good man. He was in and out of rehab most of my childhood, trying to cure himself of his vices. And every Christmas, you could find him outside of a grocery store or a mall, red Santa hat on in the freezing cold, ringing this very bell, asking for donations from the passing customers. Aside from the random good Samaritan or bored retiree, those bellringers, those lost souls, they're all ex-alkies and ex-druggies trying to better their lives. I know because I rang the bell for many years myself. It's a tight-knit community–the only thing ex-addicts like more than booze and drugs are meetings. We met twice a week. We knew each other. We were family to each other—a *fucked up* family, but family nonetheless. I lost a lot of friends over the years—just like I lost my dad. Here today, then *poof,* gone."

The old man took a deep, haggard breath, and his shoulders sank a little. His eyes gleamed madly in the light of the kitchen.

"Of course, the police said he must have just run off—and who would really give a shit, hmm? He was a deadbeat as far as his creditors were concerned. We were just another dirt-poor family in a dirt-poor, rundown neighborhood. Good riddance to bad trash, most people said."

"You took my father from me and my mother—you *stole* him from us, you bastards! And all those bells out there, each and every one of them belonged to someone else you've taken, another life drained, another family you destroyed. You go around picking off the most vulnerable people in our society, those least likely to be missed. You take something good, and you poison it. I've been watching you for a long time; I know what you are. And I've come to end you, to end all of this. I have a stake for each and every one of your murderous hearts. Vampires have no place in this city–especially at Christmastime."

The family was silent. They looked to each other and to the frail, old man, to the glittering gold bell and the silver cross he held. He stood as defiant and resplendent as a statue of a saint, an avenging angel come to this world to demand retribution. They'd underestimated him.

Then Grandma Marie laughed, and everyone turned. She was standing in the doorway of the kitchen and the living room, arms across her stomach, her head bent toward the floor. Great, big rumbling belly laughs shook her shoulders, and then she threw her head back and really howled. The others glanced at each other, and soon they were laughing too, chuckling uncomfortably to each other. All but Martin, who looked like he might be sick.

"Stop it!" he yelled. "Stop it, you fiends! I'll burn every last one of you!" But you could see in his eyes that it was too late for anything to stop.

"Oh, for heaven's sake!" Grandma Marie gasped when she finished laughing. She wiped at the tears that had gathered behind her glasses. She pushed her way through her family, sucking her teeth as she went. She stood before Martin with her hands on her hips and she stared him down. She reached out and grabbed the crucifix in his hand. He was too stunned to react. "We're not vampires, you foolish old man," she said, wrenching the cross free. She threw it to the ground, and the iron Jesus broke off with a *snap* and clattered onto the floor. "We're witches."

A steel-handled meat tenderizer swung out from behind the refrigerator and hit Martin squarely on the back of his head. His skull caved in with a crack like a busted walnut. His body wobbled to the floor, his brain already leaking out to mix with Terry's blood.

"Took you long enough, Tiffany," Grandma said.

A teenaged girl, her blonde hair tied up into pigtails with red and green ribbons, stepped out from behind the refrigerator. She blushed and smiled and looked to the floor. "Sorry, Grandma. It was so exciting, I–I didn't want it to end. They hardly ever put up a fight!"

Grandma harumphed, but she was smiling too. "I suppose there's no harm done." She kicked at Terry's corpse, and a splatter of blood painted the side of the cabinets. "Your Uncle Terry won't be too happy with you, though. He's had that heart for a very long time. And this one here is even older!" She sighed. They *had* been hoping Shannon would bring home a younger boy this year. Well, it couldn't be helped. Beggars can't be choosers. It would just have to do. "You're lucky it's still warm, young lady." She looked down at Martin's crumpled form and frowned. Almost to herself, she murmured, "He *was* handsome, you bet. Just like his father."

Grandma Marie looked around the kitchen.

Everyone stared at her, unmoving. "Well, come on! What are you waiting for?" She grabbed the handbell from Martin's hand and the Santa hat from off of his head. She handed them to Will. "Go put this back on the shelf, and go hang this hat with the others–maybe you can find a spot next to his father's. When you're done, get as much of that blood up as you can. We'll need it for the reanimation ceremony. Tommy, go get me my implements out of the closet. We'll need to get that heart out while the blood is still singing." She turned to Shannon. "My dear, won't you come over here and help your sister? Tiffany has been doing a fine job in the kitchen this year, but she doesn't have your experience yet. Maybe you can show her how to crack a ribcage without spoiling any of the meat?"

"I'd love to," Shannon said, walking across the kitchen. She put her arm around the older woman's shoulders. "Sorry he caused such a scene, Grandma. I didn't think he'd be that difficult, really. Such a weak creature. I figured he'd welcome a chance to be put out of his misery. I guess you can't judge a book by its cover. Thanks for taking care of him."

A black cat tiptoed over to where Terry lay and began licking at the congealing blood around the wooden stake in his chest. Grandma smiled warmly. She patted Shannon's hand. "Of course, my dear, of course. That's what family is for, isn't it? And if you can't count on your family, then who can you really count on? Especially around the holidays." Tommy walked back into the kitchen carrying a bag that clanked with every step, forceps and clamps and bone saws with serrated teeth jostling against each other, the ringing sound as sweet as sleigh bells in their ears.

Before the door swung shut, a few snatches of *Last Christmas* by George Michael floated into the kitchen, and they all smiled. It was their favorite Christmas song.

THE HAUNTING OF SARAH BRENDLE
ALAINE GREYSON

It began at the age of eight—the haunting of Sarah Brendle as some said. The ghosts that inhabited the small town of Holman seemed drawn to the young child. The spirits spoke to her, had tea and crumpets with her, and were constant companions. Sarah treated them as good friends, sharing their thoughts with whomever they met. Even if those thoughts weren't kind. Sarah's ice blue eyes and long blonde hair lent an air of innocence. And allowed most to laugh at the ignorant comments. But those who spent the majority of their time with the child often grew tired of the strange happenings and inappropriate comments.

"Blue isn't your color," Sarah told her nanny, only the fifth to work for the Brendle's since Sarah's gift manifested.

"Rather presumptuous for a child. Mind your manners."

"Harriet made me say it." Sarah placed her porcelain doll in the highchair next to her table and reached for the plastic tea kettle.

The nanny stared at the doll. "Harriet, that's not nice."

Sarah covered her mouth and giggled. "That's not Harriet."

"Are you referring to one of your ghost friends again? I should have listened when I was warned about this place."

Sarah glanced at her doll and smiled. "Harriet could be my doll if you wanted her to be. She can be anything if I ask her."

Nanny smirked. "Fantasies of a disturbed child." She waltzed over to Sarah's bed and pulled the sheets taut.

Sarah winked at her doll and turned toward her bookshelf, choosing her latest pony novel, and settled into a purple beanbag. Half reading, half watching, a smile formed as Harriet performed as Sarah had wished.

"A mental hospital, that's where you belong. Talking to ghosts, claiming to control them, hogwash. It's all in your mentally disturbed ..." Nanny's face turned ashen. Sarah's doll, left in the highchair, peeked out from the covers. "No." She shook her head and slapped herself across the face. "Just a figment of my imagination. The little imp is rubbing off on me."

"Something wrong, Nanny?" Sarah asked.

Nanny grabbed the doll and threw it across the room. "You have too many dolls. We should think of donating them. You're getting too old for such playthings." "Are my dolls bothering you, Nanny?"

"Not at all." Nanny turned toward the bed and adjusted the pillows. "They're just dolls."

Sarah laughed. "Yes, Nanny. Just dolls."

Nanny bent down and gathered random toys and clothes from the floor. Her eyes grew round as the items fell from her hands.

"Are you sure everything is okay, Nanny? Is my imagination rubbing off on you?"

"Whatever you are doing, make it stop."

"Make what stop? I don't see anything."

"You don't see that?" Nanny pointed a shaky finger at Sarah's doll, the same one from the highchair and the bed, now standing on the floor, crazed eyes and holding a steak knife.

Sarah trotted over and grabbed the doll, holding it to her chest. "There you are. Naughty baby. I put you in the highchair, remember?"

"The knife, Sarah."

"Knife?" Sarah removed a plastic knife from the dolls hand and held it toward Nanny. "This? A plastic knife can't hurt ... much."

Nanny backed away, and when she reached the bedroom door, tore off down the hall, down the spiral staircase and out the front door.

Sarah grinned. "Nice job, Harriet. We scared another Nanny." She held the doll to her ear. "Yes. Now it's only you and me."

The doll, now in the highchair with a cup of tea, smiled.

Other spirits communicated with Sarah, but only Harriet was her constant companion. They shared breakfast and dinner. They played together and watched television together. They had tea parties and picnics with Sarah's dolls and stuffed animals. While Harriet spooked nannies and servants, Sarah found her a trusted friend. And a defense against overbearing adults. Her parents brushed it off as an overactive imagination. Eight was a bit old to have an imaginary friend, but Sarah was isolated in her large family home with little interaction outside her family and servants. And attributing her strange conversations to someone who didn't exist was better than admitting the truth. Their denial worked. Until the spirits that followed Sarah became agitated and out of control.

The winter Sarah turned twelve, everything changed. Sarah's parents, still in denial about their daughters gift, had planned a visit to Spandau Zitadelle, a famous haunted house in Berlin, Germany. Perhaps her parents believed the inhabitants would scare Sarah and convince her to give up her silly game. Or perhaps they believed the ghosts traveling with their daughter would find a new home and depart. Whatever their reasoning, a strange occurrence set Sarah on a different path. Upon entering the castle, she sensed the change in energy. Harriet, normally chattering in Sarah's head, grew silent. The more Sarah tried to engage her childhood friend, the more she retreated.

"Harriet. Harriet. I know you're here. I can still feel you." Sarah crept down the hallway behind her parents. "It's okay, Harriet. We won't be here long and then everything will go back to the way it was."

"Hurry along, dear. The tour is starting soon. Making a grand entrance is one thing, but we can't join in once they leave this floor."

"Coming, mother." Sarah rubbed arms and cast a furtive glance toward the end of the hall. Something sinister waited. She could feel it. Whatever it was had silenced her best friend. If she turned and walked out, would Harriet's presence strengthen? Sarah drew a breath and looked behind her toward the front door.

"Sarah! Come on, child." Caroline Brendle yanked Sarah's elbow and pulled her down the hallway, stopping in front of the grand staircase. "Stop with your games."

"They're not games. Something isn't right."

Caroline motioned toward Emmett Brendle, who shrugged and buried his head in the castle's shiny brochure.

"Leave the drama and try to enjoy this trip?"

Sarah sighed. Her mother didn't understand. Harriet wouldn't disappear unless something—or someone—made her. This trip was a mistake. But Sarah was stuck and now Harriet was missing.

Emmett Brendle, his face buried in the latest issue of Rolling Stone, stood at the bottom of the staircase. Ever the absent father even when he was physically present, he murmured something and proceeded up the steps.

"What did he say?" Sarah asked.

"Just follow him. The tour guides must be waiting at the top of the stairs."

"Or the ghosts scared them off too." Sarah mumbled half to herself.

Caroline rolled her eyes and sighed. Then, setting sights on her husband, marched up the staircase.

Sarah placed a wary foot on the bottom step. "Harriet. Harriet! Where are you? It's bad form to disappear without a warning. Harriet!"

As Sarah climbed the stairs, a fog descended, shrouding her view. It wasn't a waft of cold air, or a powerful breeze. The fog hung warm and damp between Sarah and her parents. Whatever lay ahead, Sarah couldn't decipher it. She tentatively took a step forward, the feeling of companionship and playfulness she felt with Harriet replaced with doom and fear. What was this place and who lived here?

"Harriet. I'm warning you. No tea parties for a week if you don't show yourself. Harriet!"

Sarah continued up the staircase, one step at a time, feeling her way through the pea soup fog. She had never experienced a haunting like this before. Something sinister was afoot. Something that had silenced Harriet. A different voice fought to replace her dear friend. Shrill and demanding, the voice entered Sarah's mind in garbled speech, as if someone had tried to block it. "That's it Harriet. Fight them off. No one can separate us. Tell the spirit to go away."

Sarah's mind, and Harriet's will, struggled to fend off the invading spirit. Without a spoken word, the three engaged in a battle, the spirit attaching itself to Sarah like a magnet. Concentrating on Harriet, Sarah tried expelling the ghost. She closed her eyes tight and rubbed her temples. The spirit's strength proved stronger than the twelve-year-old and her ghost companion combined.

Through the fog, Sarah heard muffled voices. Her parents, the tour guide and other guests conversed as if the commotion on the steps did not exist. Sarah squinted, trying to make out the clouded figures. But the pull became too much. With a blood-curdling scream, Sarah gave in, the voice of Theresa replacing Harriet. Sarah's eyes, bloodshot and puffy, stared wide into the gathered crowd. As an orchestra played "God Rest Ye Merry Gentlemen" and the guests gathered around a large Christmas tree, Sarah fainted. The spirit of Spandau Zitadelle had won.

Theresa claimed Sarah, her will overpowering the pre-teen. And although Sarah had tried to separate from her new 'friend', Theresa refused to leave, following the family across the ocean and back to their lonely mansion in the States.

At first, Theresa's influence provided entertainment. It

wasn't the normal like flying objects or items falling from the sky. No one saw floating sheets or whisps of smoke. It wasn't like a movie, like a poltergeist in her television. It was deeper. More sinister and psychological. They invaded her mind, spoke to her as if they were one, connected somehow. As if Theresa wanted something only Sarah could provide. But she wasn't forthcoming with demands. Sarah fought daily to maintain control of her mind and actions. And control of Theresa.

Sarah's parents, frustrated at their daughter's spiraling mental health, tried to spin the issue into something believable. After all, they had reputations to uphold. They were pillars in the creative arts community in their small town of Holman. Caroline, a celloist, was first seat in the small orchestra while Emmett worked behind the scenes composing songs. Their daughter's *gift* of communing with the paranormal proved a great parlor game, entertaining their friends at parties, until the voices became difficult to control. That was when Sarah's life changed. That was when Aunt Tilly came to stay.

It was a crisp fall afternoon the year that Sarah turned thirteen. Caroline peered in her daughter's room, hesitant to enter. "Come to my room and I'll brush your hair."

Sarah smirked. "Afraid to come in, mother?"

Caroline glanced around the room. Porcelain dolls lined the shelves, their eyes round and their mouths wide. "Afraid of your overactive imagination? Come, Sarah."

"If everything is only in my mind, why did you summon Aunt Tilly?" Caroline's younger sister Tilly had circled the world investigating paranormal activities. If anyone could solve this current problem, it was her.

"Because you can't keep a nanny and you need someone to teach you how to comport yourself."

"And Aunt Tilly, the one you always complain about and call a hellcat, is your solution?"

"Hush." Tilly grasped Sarah's arm and dragged her down the hallway. Entering Caroline's bedroom, Sarah felt fabric hit her face. "Put this on."

Her mother dressed her in a gingham dress and brushed her long auburn hair. Aunt Tilly was expected any minute and her mother wanted to present a good impression. But with all the talk of Tilly and her adventures, Sarah sensed something different, and didn't know what to expect. The voices, especially Theresa's had grown in intensity, warning of danger, but Sarah didn't understand their concern. She tried to push the invading thoughts from her mind as her mother tugged on the brush.

"Ow! That hurts mama."

"Stand still and I'll be finished quicker. I've half a mind to cut this rat's nest and give you something shorter. A nice bob cut. Not as pretty but it will save me time."

"Don't cut my hair, mama. I like it long. And Theresa says long hair is more ladylike."

"Theresa? Never mind. I don't want to hear about the people living in your head. Your aunt will take care of this problem."

"But they don't live in my head, mama. They are here, in front of you."

Caroline swatted Sarah on the butt with the brush. "Nonsense."

"But Mama, you don't seem to care when your friends are here. Parading me around like a circus freak."

Caroline furrowed her brow. "Watch your tongue. Get downstairs and act presentable. Your Aunt Tilly should arrive any minute."

Aunt Tilly. Sarah had heard stories of her aunt but had

never met her. Aunt Tilly had traveled the globe looking for adventure. She spoke several languages and possessed an extensive understanding of paranormal activity. If anyone could help Sarah, it would be Aunt Tilly.

Sarah trotted down the stairs and paced the hallway. Theresa had become agitated over the past few days. Sarah didn't understand why and Theresa never shared her reason. The ghost's anxiety built inside of Sarah, causing her to fidget with her dress and bite her nails, now partially bloody. Was Theresa afraid of Tilly? Nothing else made sense. Sarah hoped they could return to playing and reading books instead of this anxiety filled madness. Theresa had sacrificed too many of Sarah's dolls showing her angst.

Sarah harnessed her thoughts, communicating with the spirits. "Calm down. Aunt Tilly is a friend, I promise. Now stop being a nuisance and give her a chance. At least she'll believe you're real."

A waft of cold air swept over Sarah and her mind went quiet. Theresa and the others had left, though Sarah knew if wasn't for long. They would return at a safer time, after they determined Tilly's motive.

Aunt Tilly stormed into the mansion like a whirlwind. Her vibrant red hair pulled into a haphazard bun, her long wool skirt scraping the floor. She carried several bags, each bursting with clothes and other strange items. Sarah swore she saw feathers sticking out of one. Servants scurried about, trying to secure her luggage as Tilly moved briskly around the foyer. Sarah shrunk into the corner closest to the library. Would it be rude to hide in there until it was safe? Was Aunt Tilly safe? Sarah didn't know anymore.

"Where is my niece? It's about time someone in this family inherited a useful talent. Where is she? Heaven knows she'll end up a mess under Caroline's tutelage."

Caroline stood on the bottom step, leaning on the railing. "Hello, dear sister. Care to repeat that to my face?"

Tilly laughed. "Heavens no. Show me to my charge and I'll tidy everything up so you can put your head in the sand once again."

"You haven't changed. Always with the put downs."

"Not put downs. Truth. Now where is Sarah?" Tilly glanced down the hallway, her eyes settling on a slight child fiddling with her dress. "Child, you mustn't stand in the corner. You need to stand up for yourself. Otherwise, they will win." Tilly marched toward Sarah and grabbed her elbow. "If they haven't already."

Sarah gulped and glanced toward her mother, as if calling out for help. But help didn't happen. Sarah tightened her body under Aunt Tilly's grasp, but unable to escape, followed her upstairs.

"We have much to do, child. First, show me your room. I must see everything first-hand. The stories your mother relays are concerning, but I must see and not just hear. We will solve this. By Christmas, we will solve it."

The mansion became alive with decorations, Christmas music and delicious food over the following days. Sarah wandered the main hall, admiring the large Christmas tree and sampling holiday treats. She reached for a sugar cookie when it started.

"T-T-Tilly!"

The panicked screech, echoing in the hallway, caught Sarah by surprise. She placed the cookie on the plate and turned toward the doorway. Something had scared her mother. Or someone. Sarah crept across the plush carpet, not making a sound.

"Oh great. This is how she decides to introduce herself." Tilly stood, arms crossed, next to an ashen Caroline.

"Make it stop. You promised you'd fix this. Fix Sarah. Make it stop now."

Tilly rolled her eyes. "It isn't that easy. We're not dealing with a wayward child. It's a centuries old spirit wanting to cause havoc. I can't just snap my fingers and ..."

"Tilly, there's three dolls hanging from my staircase with blood ..."

Tilly stuck out a finger and scooped up some of the red substance, raising it to her mouth. "It's not blood." She licked her finger. "Ketchup. Nice touch."

"Ketchup? This is ridiculous. I'm having guests over for a holiday party. You and Sarah are confined to her room until this situation is rectified." Caroline stormed up the staircase, leaving Tilly and Sarah alone.

"Theresa, huh?" Tilly questioned.

"Looks like. Totally something she'd do."

"Well, we better think of a solution, before your mother confines us to quarters forever."

The next few weeks Aunt Tilly and Sarah were confined to Sarah's room. Sarah didn't go to school. She didn't play in the back yard, and she didn't see her parents. Tilly became guardian, teacher and companion. She had insisted isolation was necessary. The only way to determine the spirits strength and to discover its weakness. But in reality, Caroline refused them access to the house unless Sarah's mental illness—or haunting—was resolved. Caroline and Emmett gave Tilly complete freedom if it meant curing their daughter's mental illness. An illness Tilly consider a gift.

"Not everyone can talk to ghosts, m'dear."

Sarah pushed her steak around with her fork. "I wish I couldn't."

"Nonsense. It's a fine gift. Think of all the history you can learn."

"History? All Theresa wants is to create chaos."

Tilly took a drink and nodded. "Some are like that. Trauma from their living years."

"Well, I don't need to suffer from her trauma. Everything was fine when it was me and Harriet."

Tilly scrunched her eyes and bit her lip. "Harriet. She was a ghost too?"

Sarah sighed. "I told you about Harriet. Yes, she's a ghost and she was my best friend. Until Theresa took over. And then Harriet disappeared. Why can't Theresa take a hint and go back to Germany."

The table shook, tea pouring on the white tablecloth. "Yes, Theresa. I want you to go away!" Sarah slammed her fork on the table and waltzed toward the bookcase. I want things to be the way they were. Before Germany. Before Theresa. I didn't mind my gift then. But now. I can't do anything, go anywhere, without chaos following. And no one believes that Theresa is behind it. Last month, she threw a ball at Camille Brewster's head and I got detention for it. I can't live like this."

"Indeed. Seems difficult."

"So, what are you going to do about it? I mean, you're here to help, right? How do we . . ." Sarah cupped her hand to her mouth. "How do we get rid of Theresa and get Harriet back?" she whispered.

"Well, there is a way. But I can't guarantee Harriet will return."

"But you can guarantee Theresa will leave?"

Tilly reached in her bag and pulled out a black case. "We can try."

"What's that?" Sarah ran a finger along the case, intrigued by the rough texture. "Some kind of ghost trap?"

"Ghost trap? You've watched too many movies. No such thing."

"Then what is it? And how can it help?"

"I'm not promising that it can help. But it's worth a try." Tilly set the case on the small table in the middle of Sarah's bedroom. "Time to test this Theresa's strength."

"Haven't we done enough of that the past few weeks? We know she won't leave. She won't listen to reason and she won't tell us why she's here. Let's face it. I'll have to live with her presence for the rest of my life. Might as well be a hermit or something."

"Pish. Stop being dramatic and do something to change it. Your weakness allows her to stay. Stand strong. It's the only way."

The only way. Sarah mulled over Tilly's words. Perhaps standing strong was the only way. Nothing else had ever worked. Every day that had passed since Theresa invaded Sarah's mind her hold had grown stronger. Until Sarah had stopped fighting. Perhaps Tilly was right. "How do I stand strong?"

"You don't let her win. No matter how hard she tries to hold on, your mind must fight her."

"The last time I tried, I blacked out."

Tilly shrugged. "It happens."

"It happens? What if she kills me?"

"Do you really think a ghost can kill?"

"Yes. Can't they?"

Tilly tapped her chin. "I suppose it's possible."

"If she kills me, what's the point? I want her to leave. I want Harriet back. And I want to live. Can you promise any of that?"

"Darling, if you think there are any promises in life you are sorely mistaken."

Sarah crossed her arms and slumped into a chair. "If you can't promise to fix things, then why are you even here? Mother was right. You are a disappointment."

Tilly cocked an eyebrow. "Is that what Caroline says? Hmph. Disappointment indeed." She sunk into the chair across from Sarah and put her chin in her hands. "Your mother has distinct ideas about success."

"Yeah. Like actually being able to perform your job."

"Who said I couldn't perform my job? I'll have you know expelling spirits isn't exactly in my job description."

This was ridiculous. Why didn't her mother hire an expert instead of relying on her kooky sister? Was it because Caroline didn't believe Sarah was really haunted? Was Aunt Tilly a ruse, something to make Sarah believe things would change? "What is your job description, dear aunt. It can't be anything involving the paranormal."

"No?" Tilly stood and glanced in the full-length mirror next to Sarah's bed. "Is it because of my outfit? Rather plain I know." Tilly smoothed her green woolen skirt and ran her hand through her bright red hair. "Or perhaps it's my hair. Rather a fright I suspect. Too much for a medium perhaps."

"For God's sake, it's not your clothes or hair. It's your lack of knowledge, your inability to ... screw it. Just go back to whatever hellhole you crawled out of and leave me alone."

"Watch your mouth young lady. You may be frustrated by our lack of progress, but I am still your aunt."

"Whatever." Sarah grabbed a book from the shelf and settled into the window seat.

Tilly waltzed toward the table, eyeing Sarah and the silver gleam emanating from the black case. "You want guarantees niece. There are no guarantees in life." Tilly removed a silver tube from the case, running her finger along the shiny surface. "Or in death. So we have two choices." Tilly grasped another silver tube and interlocked it with the first. "We can allow Theresa and other spirits to roam free. Or we can try to remove them." As Tilly connected the third and final piece, a dense fog settled in the room. "What's your choice?"

Sarah gazed at her aunt, the fog surrounding but not touching her. Sarah rose to her feet, her voice trembling. "What is that thing?"

Tilly raised the instrument to her mouth. "This? Just a simple, ordinary flute. Nothing spectacular."

Sarah approached and reached out a hand. As she brushed it with her hand, a force pushed her back onto the floor.

"Ah. This has potential."

Sarah stood and brushed off her backside. "Potential to get us killed. Put that away. Whatever it is, Theresa doesn't like it."

"But this is what I'm talking about. Are you giving in or are you willing to fight?"

Was she willing to fight? For the past year, Theresa had control. Everything had been dictated by the spirit, leaving Sarah powerless. "I don't have the ability. She's too strong."

Tilly winked at Sarah and played a long G note. "Fight."

Sarah shook her head. *Fight?* The notion remained ridiculous. How could she fight something she couldn't see, couldn't reason or bargain?

Tilly played a long C note. The bookshelf rumbled and books flew across the room slamming against the wall. "Fight!"

The fog swirled around Sarah and Tilly. The spirit's energy grew, flinging objects around the room, almost hitting them both. Sarah placed two fingers on her temples and closed her eyes.

"That's it. Fight her. You are stronger. You can win." Tilly played note after note, Theresa becoming more powerful with each sound. "Don't let her win. Claim your headspace. Tell her she's not welcome."

Theresa's energy crashed down on Sarah, forcing her onto her knees. "She's too strong. I can't do this."

"Yes, you can. This is working out better than expected." Tilly blew on the flute.

Sarah's head throbbed. Theresa's voice reverberated in her mind. "She won't leave. She says you're a witch and she won't leave."

"Witch, huh Theresa?" Tilly chuckled. "Let's see how witchy I can be." She blew three notes on the flute, sending the fog swirling violently across the room. "Hang on. We're almost through."

Sarah opened her eyes and stared at Tilly. *Almost through.* She could do this. She could ... a strong wind blew open the window and catapulted Sarah onto the bed.

"Keep fighting, Sarah. The stronger she gets, the more desperate she becomes."

"That's what I'm afraid of!" Sarah grabbed a pillow and

wrapped it around the back of her head, covering her ears. "The buzzing noise, what is that?"

"She's distracting you. Tune it out. Remember, you are in control. She doesn't own you or this space. Drive her out."

Sarah closed her eyes and drew a deep breath. She concentrated on an image in her mind. Something from her past, her early childhood. She saw a tree in the distance, a red and white checkered picnic blanket strewn underneath. Her stuffed animals and dolls sat around the perimeter. The breeze, light and fresh, enveloped her like a warm hug. *I'm here, Sarah. I've been here all along.*

Sarah's eyes blinked open. Harriet? *Don't give in. Don't let her win.*

Harriet! Had she returned?

"Child! Concentrate! We're not rid of her yet." Tilly screamed.

"It's Harriet, Aunt Tilly. She's still here."

"Well of course she is. But right now you need to focus on Theresa. Cast her out once and for all."

Tilly played a final note on the flute as Sarah concentrated on expelling the spirit from her mind. Her eyes shut and her hands plastered to her head, Sarah summoned all her strength.

"Leave Theresa. Go back to Germany. Leave me, Harriet and my family in peace. You are not welcome."

As Tilly placed the flute onto the table, a calm fell over the room. Books, toys and pillows strewn the floor. Clothes hung from the ceiling fan. And Sarah sat cross legged on the bed, her hair a disheveled mess.

"Is she gone?"

Tilly smiled. "I believe so, m'dear. Well done." Tilly

clapped Sarah on the back and began to tidy the room. "And just in time for Christmas, as promised."

Sarah ran her fingers through her hair. Theresa had left. And Harriet had helped. Harriet, oh how she had missed her. Sarah closed her eyes and smiled, transported to the field in her mind. A picnic celebration with Harriet, her dear friend, was in order. Sarah strolled along the creek lining the field. She glanced toward the tree, expecting her friend, but instead saw a void. No picnic blanket. No stuffed animals and dolls. No Harriet.

Tilly plopped on the bed, stirring Sarah from her reverie. "Shall we celebrate with some Christmas shopping and cookies?"

Sarah flashed a half smile. Theresa had gone, but so had Harriet. "Celebrate? Yes, aunt. Let's celebrate."

MY TRUE LOVE GAVE TO ME
NICOLE WOLVERTON

Melanie Walker's front porch looked like all the others on the block—long but roomy, with a well-used wooden swing dangling from chains at one end and white wicker chairs arranged just so at the other. In the middle, a bright red door festooned with a holiday wreath made of the lushest holly and pine. Mrs. Gearhart from down the street made them special and handed them out each first of December.

But on Christmas Day, something was different: a stout tree in a dark green pot squatted on her welcome mat. Not only that, but Mrs. Gearhart's wreath was shriveled and dead.

"Must have been that hard freeze last night," said Melanie's next-door neighbor Richard from his porch. He ran a hand through his thick brown hair and offered a reassuring smile.

"Oh, did your wreath die, too?"

"No, but your house probably protected mine—you're first on the block, after all."

"Did you see someone leave this tree?"

Richard set down his red mug. "Can't say that I did. Maybe one of your students left it. Happy Christmas, by the way, Melanie. D'you have plans for today?"

Melanie's heart thumped faster. She and Richard had lived next door to each other for a few years. The day he moved in all alone it had snowed a foot, and she'd helped him cart his boxes and his furniture into his house. She'd taken to inviting him to dinner each Sunday. It was just what good neighbors do in a small town like Adrian's Pocket —although Melanie didn't invite the Gearharts or her other neighbors to meals regularly. Still, Richard would kiss her on the cheek after supper each week and head back to his house, and that was that. Another week of teaching third grade would come and go, and Melanie would hope something would change between them next weekend.

"Oh," she said, "I'm making cookies later. You're welcome to stop by—I make a sinful double chocolate spiced cookie."

A smile played at the corner of Richard's lips. "I just might take you up on that." He picked up his mug again, saluted her with it, and ranged back into his house. She watched him go. It was a nice view.

When his door clicked shut, she exhaled loudly. The house was a mess, and she couldn't even get inside to clean until the tree was out of the way. She nudged the green pot with her knee, but it wouldn't budge. She struggled and yanked until the tree was beside the door, like a sentry standing watch.

It was then she noticed the nest wedged near the trunk. She brushed the branches back to get a better look—a perfect nest of twigs, and within, a fat tawny bird with a black and white head and a bright orange beak.

"Hey, little guy," Melanie said quietly. "Someone took

your tree." She released a branch, and it shook the tree. The bird toppled out of the nest. She reached instinctively to catch it, and it landed in her hand, wriggling and cold.

She shrieked and jerked away. The bird landed on her porch with a thud and burst open just under the wing, scattering maggots like tiny grains of rice.

"You okay, Melanie?" came a voice from her steps.

She whipped around, rubbing her hand against her jeans. She could still feel the wriggling on her palm. The delivery man—Sam was his name—stood at the base of the steps, brown baseball cap clasped in his hands. He was at least ten years older than Melanie; he was one of those men that looked good in salt and pepper hair.

"Just a . . . dead bird," Melanie said, trying to catch her breath.

"That's enough to scare anyone." Sam bounded up the steps and scooped the bird—and most of the maggots—up with his clipboard. "Huh. A partridge. Rare for these parts, even if it weren't the middle of winter. Where'd he come from?"

"Someone left a tree on my front porch, and the bird was in it. You didn't deliver it, did you?"

"Not me. Just a couple of boxes left in my truck, so I wanted to get them where they needed to be on Christmas —but no live trees. Or dead birds, for that matter." He grinned rakishly. He leaned down to inspect the tree. "I'll be damned—it's a pear tree. I think you've got an admirer."

"An admirer?" Melanie said. "What kind of admirer leaves a dead bird and a tree?"

"Dead bird notwithstanding, don't you get it? It's Christmas Day—the first day of Christmas." In a lovely baritone, Sam sang softly, "On the first day of Christmas my true love gave to me a partridge in a pear tree." He seemed to blush and said, "I'm sure you've got lots of men lining up to be your true love."

"If you meet any of them, let me know." Richard certainly wasn't lining up, that's for sure. She added, "If there's a turtle dove tomorrow, I hope there aren't any maggots. Not exactly the way to a girl's heart."

"I'll see what I can do if I'm the one delivering." Sam laughed and placed a wrapped candy cane in Melanie's hand. He waved his goodbye and loped back to his delivery truck.

She saluted him with the candy cane as he drove off. He was on her mind when she removed the dead wreath from her door, and when she finally was able to wash her hands. It's a rare person who would clear off a dead bird from your porch.

By dinnertime, Melanie had forgotten the bird and the tree—but memories of Sam's warm eyes were still with her as she laid the fire in the small hearth in her living room. The wood spit and hissed as she set the crinkled newspaper on flames with the long matches she kept in a box on her mantle. The smell of sulfur competed with the smell of baked apples. It wasn't that she was fickle, but in a town as small as this one, it was better not to put all your handsome, engaging eggs in one basket.

All the houses on this block were the same, and she envisioned the Gearharts and Richard and all her other neighbors building fires of their own. Sam had an apartment across town, but perhaps he was doing this same thing, too. It was a nice thought to imagine everyone in town cozying up next to a warm fire with a book and a homemade apple dumpling.

As soon as the flames licked merrily up the chimney, her doorbell rang. She wrapped a quilt around her shoulders—if it were carolers, she'd need to stay warm while they sang. But there were no carolers on the sidewalk—and no one at her front door.

"Hello?" she called.

"Oh, sorry, Melanie." Richard popped up from the other side of the tree, still standing guard on her porch. "I smelled your fire—does the offer still stand for those sinful cookies of yours?"

"Come in." She stepped aside to admit him. "I made apple dumplings instead of cookies—hope that still sounds good."

"Definitely. Hey, did you ever find out where the tree came from?"

She shook her head and headed into the kitchen; Richard followed. "Sam—you know, the delivery driver," she said, "was in the neighborhood earlier, but he said he didn't drop it. It's been quiet all day, and there's not a note. Sam says it's a pear tree."

"I was just going to tell you the same thing. Too bad there wasn't a partridge to go with it."

She shuddered. "It's funny you said that about the partridge. There *was* a partridge in the tree—only, it was dead. It was pretty gross. But enough about that. How many dumplings do you want?" She held up a wooden spoon. "I make them out of whole apples, so they're pretty big."

"Just one, thank you—it smells great. Too bad about the partridge."

She dished a dumpling into a bowl. "Not the way to

start my Christmas, that's for sure." She handed Richard the bowl and a fork.

Her own bowl still waited in the living room. The flames from the fire barely touched the darkest corners. Melanie slid into the corner of the couch, and Richard chose a spot on the floor, nearly at her feet.

He glanced at her, his fire-lit face all shadow and angle. "How's your day been?"

"Quiet. Mostly." She didn't say that she was lonely, or that she wished her house was full of laughter and noise. Her parents had died years ago, and she had no family to speak of. Every day was quiet, and this one was no different. She smiled and said, "What about you? What was Christmas like for you this year."

"Relaxed for a bit—talked to my mom and dad."

"How are they doing?" Melanie flipped back through the meals she'd made him, their conversations. His parents lived several hours away if she recalled correctly. He'd shown her a photograph once—a short, dour-looking couple dressed in brown. Not that she would ever call them dour looking to Richard's face. They were, though. The kind of seriousness that make her assume Richard had grown up in a horrible house full of sad coldness.

"Good, good. They got on me some about not giving them any grandkids yet. My mother—she's pushy. I'm just not ready for that right now."

She smothered her expression by forking out a chunk of apple dumpling from her bowl. She'd be happy to give Richard's parents an assist, even if they *were* miserable. If she and Richard got married, she could avoid her in-laws. Other people managed it—so could she. Melanie brought the fork up to take a bite and stopped midway. The firelight caught the tines of her fork, but more than that, it caught the wriggling—tiny, white wriggling maggots, all over the chunk of apple.

She hurled her bowl and had just enough presence of mind to knock the bowl from Richard's hands. It went clanging over the hardwood floor, scattering apple, dough, and maggots as it spun.

Richard jumped to his feet. "Oh, no. Where are your paper towels?"

But she couldn't speak—maggots in her dumplings? Were the apples bad? How had the maggots even survived being baked? "No, my fault, my fault. I'm just overly tired. Baking must have taken more out of me than I realized." She took his arm with trembling hands and led him to the door. "Maybe I should just get cleaned up and go to bed."

"Oh, yeah, of course," he said. "It's late. I should have called first."

"No, you're always welcome here. I'm . . . not feeling right is all. Too much excitement, I guess."

He paused outside on the porch. "Happy Christmas, Melanie. See you tomorrow?"

She pasted a smile on her face. "Absolutely."

Maggots were still on her mind when she woke up on the day after Christmas, more so when she opened her door to find the dead bodies of two sleek birds laid atop her front steps. Several maggots writhed beneath their stiff carcasses. She imagined Sam's baritone again: *On the second day of Christmas, my true love gave me to me two turtle doves and a partridge in a pear tree.*

More 'gifts' followed—on the third day, three eviscerated hens; on the fourth day, four canary heads set up accusingly across the edge of her welcome mat. Maggots everywhere. She called the police after that, and the sheriff came. He said it was just a prank, nothing to be done but wait it out.

It was Sam himself who delivered a package for her the day after that. He put an arm around her shoulder when she told him what was happening. He even opened the box for her, poised over her kitchen sink. "You don't have to look," he said.

She shook her head. "No, thanks, I don't think I will."

He turned the parcel upside down and a tiny wooden case clunked out. Sam plucked it out of the sink—the box was dark mahogany with gold hinges and clasp. She nodded to him, and he unfastened the clasp. The hinges creaked when he opened the lid. Five gold rings were nestled in purple silk.

No maggots.

She sighed. "Well, that's one day where I don't have to clean my entire house."

"I don't mean to scare you," Sam said, "but the things in the song just keep getting bigger from here."

When Richard stopped by later, he insisted on putting in surveillance cameras for her. "You can't be too careful," he said.

He wouldn't touch the gold rings or even go near them, not that Melanie could blame him. Gold rings. Marriage. He'd told his parents he wasn't ready to settle down. But maybe she could convince him he was ready to consider the idea. It would be a true holiday miracle.

The very next day, December 30th, Melanie woke to joy. The day before Hogmanay was special in Adrian's Pocket. The entire town gathered at the park at the end of Front Street to prepare the torches used for the processional on the next night. It was always so much fun—the Historical Society ladies would serve cauldrons full of warm apple cider, and children would run around, screaming with laughter until sundown, when the party would break-up for the evening.

She bounded down the stairs to her living room, dressed warmly for the occasion, flung open her door . . . and screamed. She caught her breath and screamed again. Her porch was a slaughterhouse. Feathers and blood and egg yolks and broken shells everywhere. And on her porch swing were six geese, bellies split open, intestines dangling to the floor like wet, crimson rope. The geese were crammed wing to wing, long necks slumped, maggots crawling in the corners of their milky dead eyes.

Her screams brought out the whole block. Mrs. Benscoter, from across the street, hustled Melanie inside and made tea. Hank Abernathy from three doors down led a clean-up crew. Richard paced inside her door until the sheriff arrived, and he showed the sheriff her security footage. One moment Melanie's porch was normal, and the next moment, pure carnage. It was just suddenly . . . there.

The only good part was when Richard gathered her into his strong arms. He didn't leave her side all day at the park as they prepared the torches and watched the children play. He even took her ice skating that night at the makeshift rink outside the civic arena.

As they glided hand-in-hand, he said the words she always dreamed: "Maybe you should stay with me tonight."

She fantasized about their wedding, how perfect it would be. How she'd become best friends with his mother no matter how gloomy she was, and they'd making dumplings together every Christmas Day. Even Richard's severe-mouthed father would love her. But even as she dreamed, the seventh day of Christmas loomed—it clouded out even her happiest thoughts. Richard made up the bed in his guest bedroom and told her not to worry, but it couldn't be helped. And her dreams of a wedding dimmed when he went to bed himself without even a kiss on the forehead. She tried to will herself to sleep, but the thoughts were too loud.

She huffed and flipped onto her side. Something soft brushed beneath her cheek, like the soft flutter of wings. She tilted her head away from the pillow and brushed at her face, at her hair. And in the dim light, a sprinkle of tiny white forms fell onto the comforter.

Melanie bolted upright and flicked on the light: a dozen maggots wriggled over the blankets. She stifled a screech and whipped out of bed, pawing at her hair. Richard couldn't know. She'd brought maggots into his house—*gross*. They must have been on her all day, hiding. Or maybe *not* hiding. Maybe that's why Richard had left without a kiss, without a second glance. Horror crashed through her, competing with disgust as she frantically shook out her pajamas, then squashed every last maggot with the heel of her shoe.

When Melanie returned to her house in the morning, with only a goodbye wave from Richard, Sam's delivery truck was parked a few doors down. He stood on her porch steps, eyes bugging out of his head. A pink plastic baby pool filled with water and seven rotting swans sat on her front porch.

Melanie couldn't speak.

Sam jolted and dropped his parcel when she touched his arm. Very quietly, he sang, "On the seventh day of Christmas my true love gave to me seven swans a-swimming, six geese a-laying, five golden rings—four canary birds, three French hens, two turtledoves, and a partridge in a pear tree." He turned to her. "I'm afraid for you, Melanie."

"Me too," she said. "I don't know what to do. I don't want to miss Hogmanay, but I'm scared of what comes next if I stay here."

"Tell you what—I have a fishing cabin just outside of town," Sam said, "not too far from the lake. You're welcome to stay there. No one will find you. No one even has to know you're there. You can still go to Hogmanay that way."

Melanie shivered. "That's very kind, but I couldn't stay alone in a strange place. Not now."

"No, I guess you wouldn't want to do that." Sam pinched his lip. "How about I stick by you tonight during the Hogmanay processional, then drive you out to the cabin and have a friend of mine—she's got hair just like you—drive your car back to your house. You'll stay at the cabin, and I'll be your own personal bodyguard, just in case. Doesn't have to be long . . . just a couple of days. We'll have someone swing by tomorrow morning and every day until your admirer gets it out of his system. I'll have a word with the sheriff, see if I can't convince him to put extra patrols on your house."

It was awfully brave of Sam to offer, but running away from her house—even for a few days—seemed like too much. Too much to ask. Too much to give up. "They're getting a live feed of my security video already. Not that it helps." She gestured around.

Sam harumphed. "Look, I'll take a few pictures for the police, get this cleaned up for you. Go pack your bag, rest up a bit, and I'll pick you up this afternoon. What do you say? Until tonight we'll treat it like a normal day, like none of this ever happened."

But it wasn't a normal day. Not as Melanie paced her

house, wondering what she'd done to deserve this kind of attention, and certainly not when Sam picked her up for the processional. She smiled at her neighbors and the others in the community—except Richard, who hadn't even come to the celebration—and she dutifully took part in the torchlight parade down Front Street at midnight. But she peered into each face, wondering if it was that person who was torturing her like this. And it *was* torture. Melanie's world was nothing more than a parade of avian corpses and disgusting maggots.

Nothing was amiss, though. No one leered menacingly. No one dropped a heavy-handed hint about being her admirer. In fact, no one mentioned the horrible 'gifts' on her porch at all, as though they'd had a secret meeting without her and decided to consciously avoid bringing it up. The only indicator that she hadn't made it all up was Sam. As promised, he'd stuck by her like glue. And at the end of the night, he helped her clean up the park, along with the other neighbors. He was a true gentleman. A man of his word. And at nearly one in the morning, he hustled her away from the park to a dark nook and into the passenger seat of his delivery truck.

They passed no one along the winding road out to Sam's cabin. Lake Lokakoma sank below them in the valley, the moonlight cresting off the gentle waves and kissing the roofs of the houses that dotted the shoreline. They turned off into a heavily wooded area, the trees growing thicker with each mile, the road growing narrower until it was barely wide enough for the truck to pass. And finally, Sam turned into a driveway hidden among the pines. The driveway opened into a clearing, and in the middle of the clearing was a small log cabin with a green door.

Sam shouldered Melanie's duffel bag and helped her

out of the truck. The gravel driveway crunched under their feet, and the cold, resinous air tasted sweet to Melanie. For the first time in days, she wasn't worried about maggots or dead birds or secret, unhinged admirers. Sam led her up the slate path to the door and let her in. She stood in the dark, shivering, until the click of a light revealed the interior of the cabin: a living area with a tiny open kitchen at one end and two open doors that led to—if she had to guess—a bedroom and a bathroom.

"It's not much," Sam said, "but no one knows you're here."

The words echoed in her ears. For a moment it felt ominous, but this was Sam. She'd known him for as long as she'd lived in Adrian's Pocket. Everyone loved him. He braked for animals and delivered homemade soup when anyone was sick.

"You're safe," he said.

She grinned. Of course she was. Of course.

"You'll take the bedroom." He swept through the door and turned on a lamp inside the room. Melanie followed him in, finding it was just big enough for a large bed and a dark-wood dresser. He set her duffel bag on the russet-colored duvet and smiled. "I want you to feel at home. The bathroom is next to this room. Help yourself to anything. Shampoo. Milk. The steaks in the freezer. Anything."

"This is really so generous," she said.

"I'll stay up until morning, keep an eye out. Nothing bad will happen to you here."

And he was right. The next day there were no disgusting gifts outside, and when Melanie called the sheriff's office, he reported nothing on her own porch either. Maybe the new year had broken the pattern. Maybe whoever it was who'd been doing this had lost interest.

Whatever the case, the next few days were the most relaxing of Melanie's life. She lounged on Sam's overstuffed plaid couch during the day while he slept in the bedroom. She made them both dinner every night. And he patrolled. And on the eleventh day of Christmas she kissed him, square on the mouth. He'd smiled and kissed her back.

She did wonder whether Richard even noticed she was gone. She imagined that he'd been so disgusted with the maggots in her hair that he'd sold his house and moved out of town—but that was just a fantasy. She'd have to face him sooner or later, knowing he'd abandoned her when she needed him. Maybe it was better that he wasn't ready to settle down. And she did have Sam now.

That night, Sam dropped Melanie off at her house. Her perfect house with the pretty white porch, identical to all the other houses on her block. They kissed in her doorway, and he handed her the duffle bag.

"Call me when you get home, okay?" she said. He nodded, grinned, and jogged down her front steps, back to his truck.

She put her clothes in the washing machine, against her better judgment—she didn't want to scrub the magic of the last few days off herself. She wanted to live in that space, in Sam's cabin, forever. *He* was the true holiday miracle. It was midnight before she realized that Sam had never called her. She rang his phone. No answer.

Maybe he'd gotten called in for an emergency delivery. It happened sometimes, he'd said—especially around the holidays. And he *had* been off from work the last few days. No matter. She smiled to herself; he wasn't the only one who could do something nice, something surprising. She would go to his apartment across town and make him a late dinner. A very late dinner. And when he got home from work there would be something waiting for him. It was the least she could do.

She slipped on her boots, thrust her arms into her coat, and shoved her keys in her pocket. She switched on her porch light, opened her front door, and froze. In the moonlight her entire porch floor wriggled as though alive.

Hung like jaunty lanterns across her porch, a row of eight young girls swung. Their toes brushed across the writhing floor. Their milky, dead eyes stared right at Melanie. Wires passed through them, ear-to-ear, holding them aloft. A silver pail sat in front of each girl, filled to the brim with more maggots. Melanie clapped her hand over her mouth, maybe to hold in a scream, maybe to hold in vomit—she wasn't sure.

Positioned in and around her wicker chairs were the broken, disjointed bodies of nine women, forced into impossible configurations. Each wore a pair of bloody pointe shoes. One of the women had hair just like hers, or at least it looked that way in the glowing moonlight.

At the bottom of Melanie's steps sprawled ten young men, their slit throats spilling now-dried blood down the front of their Adrian's Pocket High School band uniforms. A pristine white and silver bass drum rested on the stiff leg of the nearest boy. The almost human-looking skin of the drum bounced with maggots.

Planted on the edges of the front path throw her yard were eleven severed heads, lips pursed as though they were actually playing the flutes carefully placed at their chins.

Just beyond the women were a dozen men tied ankle to ankle, shoulder to shoulder, mounted on pikes to look like a chorus line of leaping sentries. This time Melanie let her scream go. It echoed in the night, bouncing off the pavement and reflecting back to her—the tallest of the men had salt and pepper hair, and he used to have the kindest smile she'd ever seen.

Her Sam.

Now his mouth, like the rest of the men, had been sliced wide to leave a gaping dark hole. She may have been twenty feet away in the middle of the night, but it was bright enough to see the white squirming mass in their mouths. She wanted to run, to flee, but her feet were frozen in place.

She screamed again and kept screaming until Richard's porch light beamed on. He emerged from his house at a run, leaping over his railing until he stopped short of the sight of her yard. His mouth opened, and she thought he might scream too, but he let out a loud, braying laugh that went on for so long that she quieted past a new and sudden spike of fear coiling in her stomach and wrapped her arms around herself.

"Mother!" he yelled. "Show yourself. Right now!"

"Richard, what are you doing?" Melanie called. "Call the police. Call . . . call everyone!" And where were her other neighbors? Why was Richard the only one to hear her? She glanced fearfully at the bodies, at the heads . . . at their familiar, neighborly faces. Oh *no*.

Richard sighed irritably. "Look, this has nothing to do with you, Melanie. Okay, it does, but . . . I swear to fucking god, Mother—how many times do I have to tell you?"

The maggots on the porch retreated, twisting together down the steps, flowing like a curtain over the bodies. Melanie's stomach lurched. She clutched at herself tighter. She caught sight of Sam's corpse again, at his open mouth, and imagined his baritone, singing merrily, "On the first day of Christmas my true love gave to me . . ."

The congealed horde of maggots formed a tower, and the tower formed arms and legs, a torso and a head. And then suddenly an older woman stood on the lawn in a prim brown dress and a tidy hat. She turned and frowned at Melanie, and Melanie gasped, her head going as light as air. She'd seen the woman before—Richard's dour mother. She was sure of it.

"I told you," the woman said to Richard. "Your father and I want grandbabies, and we want them now. We gave you the perfect opportunity here. Drove this one," she jabbed her finger at Melanie, "right into your house. She had weeks away from her classroom—ripe for the taking. All you had to do was make a move."

Melanie's legs shook; it was the only movement her body would allow. She was in shock. She had to be. This was nothing more than a hallucination.

Richard hung his head. "I'm not ready to settle down. Melanie's nice and all, but—"

"No, you had to go and ruin all of our preparation. I slaved and I slaved, and we even gave you a sign, sent the messengers that night in your guest room. What did you do? Nothing. You ignored her. And now look what you made me do. We got it all set up for you again—all you needed to do was mate with her. But *ooh* no, you come running to mommy, blaming me after all I did for you." His mother turned around and shouted at Melanie, "What's wrong with my son? He's not good enough for you? You had to go sniffing around that other man?"

The wind picked up, and it blew through the flutes, sending up a dissonant whine off the severed heads on the walk in Melanie's yard. "I . . . I . . ."

Richard's mother rolled her eyes. "Well, I certainly can't have you ruining my boy's chances with the next one."

"Mother, come on," Richard said. A moment later, as his mother burst apart into a million maggots, he looked directly at Melanie. "I'm really sorry about this. My mother can be such a pain in the ass around Christmas." He turned away and walked back to his porch.

A tide of maggots raced for Melanie. She couldn't move. Couldn't run. All Melanie could do was close her eyes and hum "and a partridge in a pear tree" to block the sound of the maggots coming nearer and nearer.

SARAH BRENDLE: THE END?
ALAINE GREYSON

"God rest ye merry gentlemen, let nothing you dismay." The words rang out as Sarah Brendle deftly played the tune on her sterling silver Yamaha flute. As the Christmas chorus sang, other instruments joined, resounding in a joyous crescendo that reverberated against the music hall rafters. Sarah kept the pace set by the violins and cellos, her foot involuntarily tapping to the rhythm. Her final performance with Holman's orchestra, the only professional orchestra in the deep south, had gone to plan. No mistakes or missed notes. Sarah had even nailed the staccato that had eluded her through hours of rehearsal. Maybe it was the joy of the season, or maybe it was relief knowing she was leaving this part of her life behind for good.

Tomorrow morning began a new adventure, far from Holman, it's demands and disappointments. And hopefully, far from the memories and pain that had plagued her the last year. Pain that she thought had been eradicated twelve years ago. Yes, running away to the mountains—did she say running away? Moving to her aunt's estate in the Black

"

Mountains was the change she needed. Only Edward, Sarah's ex-boyfriend, called it running away, but what did he know?

The audience stood as the song ended, giving the orchestra a standing ovation. Sarah's hands trembled as she lowered her instrument and stared into the crowd. She was happy, relieved, that her performing life had come to an end. The rehearsals and demands would cease and her life would regain the tranquility she missed. And the haunting secret she had kept from her colleagues and friends would resolve. Yes, Tilly remained her only hope, and her only chance at sanity and survival.

Sarah's eyes darted around the music hall as memories flooded her mind. She *was* relieved. She wouldn't miss this. A tentative smile formed as she took a small bow and turned toward the back of the stage. She wouldn't miss the spotlight. A calm, tranquil life was all she needed, far from Holman. And far from *her*.

"Decent set, Sarah. A bit sharp on the chorus." Edward Strong smirked as he placed his violin in its case. "You're bound to go rusty hiding in those mountains, without me to push you."

Push her? Is that what he thought? Sarah supposed there was some truth to his words since Edward had pushed her toward accepting her aunt's invitation. Not in a friendly way, but in an 'I've got to get away from his toxic behavior' way. Behavior that he refused to own. "I don't need your help. You've done enough to derail my life."

"Derail your life? That's comical. I thought I *was* your life. That's what you said in Paris."

At one time, Sarah thought Edward was the one, her soulmate. They had plans to travel the world, playing for dignitaries across the globe. Until that night. That dreadful night. "I was naïve and stupid. Germany proved that."

"Germany proved you an amateur and an immature girl."

"Germany proved you an unsympathetic, selfish jerk."

"Because I don't believe that some Victorian German ghost is haunting you?"

Edward didn't believe in Theresa. The lack of trust and accusations of drama and lying were too much. Nothing convinced Edward of the truth.

"You don't trust me. Why would I lie about it?"

"Why would you lie? Because you're certifiably crazy? Insane? You need an asylum, not your aunt's mansion."

Sarah's breath caught in her throat. Always with the insults, Edward would never change. It was best they parted ways for good. And her adventure into the Black Mountains provided the opportunity.

"No response? You realize what you're giving up? The orchestra won't save your spot. And by the time you realize your mistake, you'll be out of touch and incapable of performing at this level again. All because ..."

Sarah's eyes grew round. "Stuff it, Edward. You have no right to judge my decisions or try to dictate my life. And you've no right to an explanation."

Edward lowered his violin case to the floor and approached Sarah. "Watch your tone." His eyes darted around the room. "And watch your back."

"Watch my back? Is that a threat?"

Edward's face inched closer, his breath hot on her cheek. "Threat, promise, is there a difference?"

Sarah flinched. What was Edward's game? Did their breakup drive him mad? Why else would he threaten her? Whatever his reason, this solidified her decision. The mountain retreat, starting life over with her aunt and leaving music and Edward behind remained her best choice. Only Aunt Tilly believed her secret since she had seen the spirit at work and had defeated her the first time. Edward believed Sarah had gone insane during their Germany trip. He never listened or believed her stories about spirits haunting her since childhood. Knowing the risks, he insisted on the trip, dismissing her claims as drama and childish imaginations. Even seeing the results of that trip, he still denied Sarah's claims. She breathed deeply, then turned and marched toward the music hall exit.

"Good luck hiding in the mountains, darling. It takes real courage to run from your mistakes instead of fixing them. But then, you've always been a scaredy cat."

Edward's words, loud for all to hear, temporarily paralyzed Sarah. Her hand balled into a fist, her cheeks turned bright red, as she processed the words. Scaredy cat. This wasn't the first time that Edward had used those words. Sarah faced him, her eyes round. "Don't. That night in Germany—"

"Yes? What about that night in Germany? Ready to tell the truth instead of sticking with your crazy story? Haunted by a ghost, ha! We were scheduled to play a private affair. And you took off. No explanation. You disappeared and left me to explain."

"You agreed to a performance at a haunted castle."

"At Halloween. Isn't that the point? A haunted Halloween performance. Besides, it wasn't *really* haunted."

Sarah shook her head, refusing to believe his stupidity. "Spandau Zitadelle is a famous haunted house in Berlin. Everyone knows it's haunted."

"Everyone who believes in superstition."

"Everyone who has ever been in the castle—"

"I was there for two hours and saw nothing. Face it. You were scared to perform without the crutch of the orchestra. And now you are running away and hiding in the mountains."

"You've said that. Repeatedly. You accused me of running away when you embarrassed me in Germany. Now you accuse me of running away again. Protecting my sanity isn't running away."

"So you admit you're insane?"

Sarah stared, steely eyed, at Edward. "I know what I saw at that castle. I've known since I visited as a child. You saw her. You experienced her wrath. Why you insist on denying it, why your disbelief trumps our relationship, I will never understand."

"It was a Halloween party. It's supposed to be spooky. Parlor games, special effects, that's all. There's no such thing as ghosts."

Sarah closed her eyes and sighed. No such thing as ghosts. Ha. Edward can believe what he wishes, but Sarah knew the truth. And the ghosts had done her a favor, showing Edward's true self before she had committed her life to him. She turned and marched out the exit into the crisp night air. It was time. Time to leave this town and Edward behind her and see what her aunt and the peaceful mountains had in store. And time to defeat Theresa once and for all.

Two days later, Sarah stood outside her Aunt Tilly's estate, in the heart of the Black Mountains. She had only visited a few times, but the smell of the pellet stove, the pine from the forest of trees surrounding her property and the sound of birds chirping brought back memories. This was the retreat Sarah had sought. No rehearsals, no dignitaries to entertain, no Edward, and no spooky castles. Yes, spending Christmas, and possibly more, would be the cure to set her back on track. And possibly toward a new future. A future without Theresa. Sarah drew a breath and stared at the massive Victorian home.

"You gonna stare or go inside?"

Sarah startled, not expecting the deep, grainy voice that seemed to come from nowhere. Standing between two massive green hedges stood a man with flowing white hair under a green woolen hat and wrinkly skin, possibly from too much time in the sun. "I'm Tilly's niece, Sarah."

"I didn't ask your name, child. I already knew that. You going in or what?"

Sarah glanced at the ground and fumbled with her keys. "Yes. Just need to get my bags." She turned toward the car.

The old man hobbled toward her and placed a hand on the car door. "Let me. Go see your aunt. She's waiting for you."

"Thank you, um, whoever you are. But I can get my things." Sarah reached for her suitcase, knocking her flute case to the car floor.

"Nonsense. You're Tilly's guest. Guests don't carry their own things. Especially ladies." His gnarled fingers clasped her suitcase and pulled it from the backseat. "What about that thing?" He pointed toward the flute case.

Sarah shook her head and closed the car door. "Not important. I don't even know why I brought it."

He shrugged and heaved the suitcase toward the house. "Whatever you say. This way. Tilly is waiting in the Christmas room."

Christmas room? Sarah smiled. A room full of tidings of

great joy instead of ghosts and Halloween decorations sounded peaceful and delightful. Something she needed after living with Edward and his horror show. Sarah followed the old man through the front door and toward the back of the house.

"Mind the porcelain. Tilly has it just so." The old man dragged the suitcase through the hall and deposited at the bottom of the stairs.

There was something familiar about the old man, but Sarah couldn't place him. His eyes, a steely gray, reminded her of someone. She pushed the thought aside and concentrated on the task in front of her.

Aunt Tilly had summoned her not only for an escape, but another attempt to get rid of Theresa. This time, Sarah wanted her gone for good. Where did spirits go when they were exorcised? Hopefully, Aunt Tilly had a plan that would be quick and painless.

Sarah surveyed the hallway, full of shelves stacked with porcelain dolls of all sizes. It reminded her of a girls playroom. Dolls dressed in play clothes, elaborate dresses and Christmas outfits lined the walls. "I didn't know Aunt Tilly collected dolls."

"Collected? Hmph. That's a word you could use."

"It is an extensive collection. I imagine they are worth quite a bit."

The old man mumbled. "Worth better dead than alive."

Sarah froze and stared at the strange old man. What did he know? Had he experienced the spirits? Living with Tilly, it was possible. Maybe he would understand Sarah and not judge like so many others had through the past year. A slight smile crept across her face. "Is Christmas a big thing for my aunt? I don't remember her caring much one way or the other."

"You could say that. Keeps the evil spirits away."

"Evil spirits? What do you know of evil spirits?"

His eyes widened as he leaned close. "What do you know of evil spirits, Miss? The uneasiness in my belly says you know more than you're telling."

Sarah's face turned ashen. Was Theresa's presence evident, even here? "Do you sense something?"

"Should I?"

Sarah gulped. "No, of course not. Thank you. I'll find my aunt from here."

He nodded toward her flute case. "'Whatever you're hiding, hun, you'll need that flute. Keep it close. It could come down to life or death."

Sarah froze. *Life or death?* Theresa had been a nuisance twelve years ago. And remained the same over the past year. But she had never threatened Sarah. She wanted to ask what he knew about the spirits and their haunting. Perhaps he had wisdom Tilly didn't. Perhaps he could control Theresa. Perhaps ...

A window blew opened and a cold draft swirled around the hall. Sarah felt Theresa smile as if greeting old friends. A fog settled in front of her. Whatever Aunt Tilly had planned for this exorcism, Theresa and the other spirits were prepared for a fight.

"What do you know about spirits and haunting?" Sarah glanced toward where the old man had stood. Vanished without a trace. Sarah closed her eyes and gathered her courage. Aunt Tilly had the answers.

She marched down the hallway, clutching her flute case, determined to end the haunting once and for all. This time, it wasn't enough to send Theresa back to Spandau Zitadelle. She needed to be cast off the earth, into whatever abyss spirits belonged. But how to make that happen eluded her.

The paranormal energy increased with every step toward the Christmas room. The porcelain dolls lining the hallway followed Sarah with their eyes, smiles creeping on their tattered faces. *Go away, Theresa. We beat you before, we can beat you again.* Sarah spoke to the ghost in her head, only to be met with cackling and disdain.

You almost ruined my life when I was twelve. And for the past year you've been a nuisance. But that ends. I want my life back, Theresa.

"Of course you do, dear. That's why you're here. Now stop dilly dallying and let's get to work."

Sarah's mouth hung agape. Aunt Tilly appeared a few feet in front of Sarah, her once auburn hair now gray. Tilly's style sense had not changed, still favoring long woolen skirts and sweaters. Her face, wrinkled and worn, still conveyed kindness and wisdom. A sense of calm and relief fell over Sarah as she embraced her aunt.

"It's been too long. I'm sorry I'm visiting under these circumstances. I wish it were different. Wish I was different."

"You are different, child. But not like you think. You are different in the way you were meant to be different. No two people are the same. And not many have your gift."

Sarah shook her head. "You've called it a gift my entire life. But it's never felt like a gift. It ruined my childhood. It ruined my career and my relationships. What kind of a gift does that?"

"Come. We've much to discuss. And you've much to learn."

❄

Sarah awoke the next morning to buzzing and the smell of fresh cut grass. Throwing off the covers, she strolled toward the window and peeked into the backyard. Snow that had covered the ground last night magically melted. Lush green grass, trimmed hedges and tall oak trees littered the yard. Had she slept past Christmas and woken in the spring? Sarah shook her head, trying to make sense of the scene.

In the corner of the yard, the old man who had greeted her last night stood, his overalls covered in dirt and grass clippings. Sarah pushed open the window and leaned out her head. "What'd you to do the snow? Looks like spring out here."

The old man gave her a cursory nod and returned to his work. Sarah remained convinced that he knew more than he let on, and she resolved herself to discovering what he knew. Perhaps he had a special knowledge into the spirit world that even Aunt Tilly didn't possess. Her aunt had hired him for some reason, and it wasn't like Tilly to hire help unless they served a deeper purpose.

Whatever his involvement, it would have to wait. Sarah pulled on a robe and slid into her slippers. Before she could tackle this mystery and the old man, her stomach demanded food. She hoped Aunt Tilly had hired a chef along with the old man. Otherwise breakfast could be slim.

Sarah sashayed down the hallway, her robe swaying against her legs and her head held high. If any spirits wished to mess with her today, they would be met with confidence and strength.

The spiral staircase led to foyer, where Sarah had first entered mere hours prior. She remembered the dark paneling, red carpet, and porcelain dolls lining the walls. In the dark, the scene set an ominous tone. In the daylight, the décor came alive with gold tint on the walls and silver thread gleaming from the carpet. The dolls, whose eyes had created an uneasy feeling last night, added whimsy and cheer. Sarah bit her lip, her mind racing. Were the spirits stronger at night?

"Stop dawdling and get in here."

Sarah focused on the petite figure in front of her. "I hope you have breakfast ready, Aunt Tilly. I'm starving."

Tilly waved her hand and marched into the kitchen. "It's nothing fancy but it will get us through."

The kitchen island teemed with fruit, cereal, a gallon of milk and assorted yogurts. It wasn't fancy, but Sarah's stomach would settle for anything. She plopped into a bar stool and poured some oat cereal into a bowl. "Who's the old man?"

"Old man? Whatever are you talking about?"

"The old man who works for you. He carried in my luggage last night and this morning he was cutting the grass in the backyard."

Tilly chuckled. "Cutting grass? After it snowed two feet last night?"

"It didn't snow. As a matter of fact, all the snow is melted. I saw it. The air smelled like fresh cut grass. The old man was covered in dirt and grass clippings."

"This is more serious than I thought. Theresa only appears in your mind, right? You've never seen an apparition?"

"No. Even Harriet existed in my head. Not that she wasn't real."

"Yes, dear. We know that Harriet and Theresa are real spirits. But the old man, this is new. You're now seeing ghosts, not just feeling and communicating with them."

"So you're saying he's a ghost? A spirit like Theresa?"

"Well, I haven't hired a soul and no one else lives here but me."

Sarah bit her lip. "But he mentioned your name. He knows you."

"And that makes him alive and not a ghost? Theresa knew your name from the start."

It didn't make sense. How could a ghost present as a flesh and blood human? He even carried her bags into the house. Spirits could inhabit objects and people, but they couldn't carry objects like the old man had done. Aunt Tilly was becoming senile. That was the only explanation.

"The next time you see this apparition, tell me. Now we have two ghosts to eradicate."

"I hate to tell you this, but there are more spirits in this house than you think. I can feel their energy."

Tilly pulled back her stringy gray hair. "Yes, darling. I'm aware. But we're concerned with disruptive spirits. The friendly ones can stay."

The friendly ones. After Theresa's influence Sarah doubted any of the ghosts would remain friendly. "The last time Theresa attached herself to me, you used a special flute to make her leave."

"Did I? Special flute you say?" Tilly stroked her chin. "Don't recall a special flute. Perhaps your flute will work?"

"You had that one with the textured black box. You said it was special. When you played it, I forced her from my mind."

"So, was it the flute or you dear?" Tilly breezed past Sarah into the Christmas room. "Come along, best to strike when you have your rest. Fighting off spirits is exhausting."

❄

The morning passed without incident. Theresa was quiet and the old man didn't appear. Maybe she did imagine him. The result of a stressed mind, filling in holes and making things up to distract herself. She settled into the armchair and gazed at the giant Christmas tree. If she focused on Tilly and the holidays, maybe Theresa and the other bothersome ghosts would disappear.

"Why are you and I so different? Mom and Dad never heard ghosts. Why us?"

"Curiosity."

Sarah shook her head. "I don't understand. This gift makes me a curiosity. People believe I'm mad. Edward threatened to have me committed."

"Bah! Edward is the one who needs committing."

"Aunt Tilly! It's difficult for people to understand. Spirits that talk to you, but don't appear? Ghosts that invade your mind? It sounds like a mental illness. I'm sure he's ..."

Tilly flashed a sly smile. "Defending him are you? I thought you hated him."

"I don't know. Everything was great until Theresa found me again."

"Then we get rid of her and you can return to your life in Holman."

"No. That's over." Sarah rose and walked toward the tree. She fingered the tinsel as a single tear welled in her eye. "She's taken everything. My life, my sanity, my career ..."

"And you let her."

Sarah pursed her lips. "Is that what you think? I let her?"

"Yes. And if you don't fight like I made you last time, she will win. And this time, she'll take your life."

A waft of hot air blew into the room. Sarah shuddered. "She's here."

"Of course she's here. She hasn't left you. But she's strongest when you're at your most vulnerable. When you give in to your emotions, she feeds off them and her power grows. You have to fight."

"I can't."

"Can't or won't?"

Sarah closed her eyes and placed her head in her hands. "I can't. She's been in control for a year. Last time, it was a few weeks. She knows my weakness."

"You know what? You're right. You can't beat her. I don't know why you even came. She's a part of you. May you live happily ever after." Tilly marched out of the room.

"Wait! Aunt Tilly! You have to help me!"

Great. Without Tilly's help Theresa would win. Sarah couldn't defeat her on her own. *Stop cackling you dead witch.* She sunk into the armchair and covered her ears, like that stopped Theresa from invading her mind.

"Help!"

Sarah jolted up and glanced around the room. The voice wasn't Theresa's. And it wasn't Tilly's. She crept toward the hallway, trying to decipher where the voice emanated.

"Okay, okay. I believe you now. Please help!"

The decidedly male voice sounded familiar. But it couldn't be. Sarah tiptoed into the hallway and glanced into the library. The scene was classic Theresa. But it didn't make sense. What was he doing here and why was he dressed like ...?

"Why didn't you warn me?"

"Why are you here? And dressed like that?"

Edward, pinned to wall by knives, stared at Sarah and grinned. "You look nice."

"Ummm ... thank you?"

"No problem. Now can you help me down?"

"Not until you explain yourself. What are you doing here?" Sarah reached for the green wool hat laying next to him. "It was you."

Edward flashed an uneasy smile. "Surprised?"

"You followed me and impersonated an old man? Why?" Sarah threw the hat on the floor. "No, don't answer that. Aunt Tilly thought you were a ghost. She had me believing my *gift* summoned you. I started questioning my sanity. But it was you. This is a new low, Edward."

"I get it. Just help me down, okay?"

"Not yet. Why, Edward?"

His face softened as their eyes met. "Because I love you, Sarah. And I needed to know the truth. Needed to be there and help you if you needed me."

"You love me? I should believe that after the way you've treated me? You weren't kind before I left."

"I was a jerk. After you left, I felt awful. Everything I said was out of fear and ignorance. I know now. I've experienced her and I know the struggle. I'm sorry I ever took you to the castle. I should have listened to you."

"Yes, you should have."

"Can you get me down and then we can talk?"

Sarah approached and reached for a knife. As she touched the handle, a force pushed her back onto the floor. "She says I can't free you. She says you belong to her."

"She?"

"Theresa. I thought you believed me?"

"Oh, I do, I do. Theresa, you say. Does she respond to flowers and chocolate?"

Sarah threw her head back and laughed. "Romancing a ghost? Good luck with that."

"It's worth a try. I mean, she is a woman."

"That's the most sexist thing ..."

A fog fell over the room. Theresa's voice played in Sarah's mind. *You can't win. Fight if you must, but all of this is mine. It's always been mine.*

Sarah cast a loving glance toward Edward. He had dressed as an old man and followed her. He wanted to know the truth. He loved her. Sarah reached a hand and caressed his cheek. "I wish things were different. I wish we could be together."

Edward's eyes grew round. "Darling?"

Sarah pulled a knife from the wall and traced a line around his throat. "Yes, darling?"

"What are you doing, darling? I thought we were making up?"

She laughed. "That may be, darling. Except, I'm not Sarah." She plunged the knife into his throat and cackled as blood ran down the wall and pooled on the floor.

"Deny my existence? This is your consequence. Theresa wins. Theresa always wins."

SUNSHINE FOR CHRISTMAS

L. A. STINNETT

Jessie trudged through the snow in her thick, fleece-lined winter boots decorated with pink hearts. The snow crunching beneath her tiny feet, and her singsong humming broke the silence of the deathly still evening. Bare tree branches clawed at the glowing moon; light sparkled off ice crystals blanketing the ground as soft snowflakes drifted lazily down.

Her friend was out there somewhere; he always made her play hide and seek to find him. Red-cheeked with hot, steamy breath pouring from her mouth and nose, the young girl approached a dark, snow-covered boulder. She tip-toed around the side, jumping past the edge.

"BOO!"

To her disappointment, there was nothing but an endless white field that seemed to go on forever. Her shoulders slumped in frustration. Jessie huffed; the game was only fun when she discovered him quickly. The search for her friend was lasting forever, and she was tired of this endless trek. Her toes were beginning to numb, and her calves ached from pushing through the dense snow. It wasn't fair that he was such a good hider. She'd checked the gardens and all around the outbuildings, but he was nowhere to be found. There was no trace of his passing. Only her tiny boot prints marred the pristine landscape.

"I'll give you one more chance, and then I'm going home," Jessie grumbled into the darkness, shaking her little fist in the air.

He was trying to trick her by not using the usual hiding places. The copse of tall snow-covered spruce trees was the next place to check. A lonely howl pierced the night, but she refused to fear what lurked in the shadows. Jessie turned to continue her hunt, screaming wildly at the ashen face with menacing red eyes appearing out of nowhere. His wide-open mouth displayed long, pointed fangs. He narrowed his brows at her and stuck his tongue out. She shrieked with laughter, pounding her feet excitedly at the jump scare he'd thrilled her with.

"There you are. Do you know what day it is, Mr. Syn?"

He leaned back on his heels to examine the young girl. Her full, round cheeks were chapped red from the chill air nipping at her skin. A rainbow-colored knit cap covered her golden locks, and a baby-blue puffy parka kept winter's icy tendrils from freezing his precious sunshine.

"It's just another day in my endless existence," he said in a heavy accent, with no steamy breath escaping as he spoke. To Jessie's ears, his speech sounded like the Baltic boatmen who sailed to the archipelago in the summer with supplies to sustain her family through the long winter.

"No, silly. It's Christmas Eve," she replied with a giggle.

"The god of Christmastide abandoned me long ago. I do not partake in his celebrations."

She tilted her head, squinting curiously at him. "I made

this for you." She raised her drawing. "It's my present for you."

"I am a monster. What makes you think I'm interested in a child's scribblings?"

"I drew the sun to help you remember what it looks like," she said proudly.

He held up Jessie's gift. It was crude in the way all children's drawings were, but the simple image meant more to him than all the world's riches. It'd been ages since he'd last basked in the sun's light. The precious illustration was a reminder of the humanity he'd lost. But he hadn't lost it; he'd thrown it away for the promise of power.

Long ago, he was just an ignorant, poor peasant who agreed to take on the curse of a strange, old man offering a promise to make him a god among men. He awoke from the arcane ceremony with an insatiable thirst for blood. Learning too late, he'd been tricked into becoming a creature of the night, feeding on the living to sustain his existence. He despaired in his foolishness that led him to such a wretched predicament until he began taking the lives of noblemen, living lavishly on the riches gained from his victims. He reveled in his new power for many years until the black plague swept through Europe in the 1300s, decimating the human population. At first, he attempted to feast on the blood of the diseased, but their putrid essence made him violently ill. Even now, thinking of the green-tinted blood made him nauseous. Without enough healthy humans to sustain him, he sealed himself away in the hidden ancient tomb of a disgraced king, forgotten to time.

The Harcourt family followed the old legends and discovered his crypt filled with ancient treasures. They transported him to the ice-locked archipelago prison to exploit him in his weakened state. His insight into the forgotten burial sites of bygone kings and their treasures made the Harcourts rich beyond imagination. A pact was struck to provide him with human sacrifices to bring him back to full vigor. The family vowed to care and provide for him for all time in exchange for the wealth of knowledge he possessed.

"Thank you, my dear child. You are the sunshine that brightens my day, making the eternal imprisonment bearable."

"Aren't you cold?" she said.

"No, child. The dead do not feel the chill of winter." He was grateful the frozen bodies of his recent victims lay buried beneath soft pink snow mounds so as not to scare her away. Her mere presence brought warmth to his being.

She reached out for his hand. Icy fingers grasped her purple mittens. "Come on. Let's play."

"Your parents will be very displeased if they find you out here, Jessica Marie Harcourt."

"It's Christmas Eve, remember. They're asleep already."

"As you should be too, Jessie," he said sternly, rising gracefully to his feet.

"I'm too excited. Do you think we'll see Santa flying to my house?" she said, flopping onto her back and waving her arms and legs to create a snow angel. Starlight shimmered in the deep brown pools of her eyes, dilating wide in the darkness. She gazed up at the vast constellations above, singing, "Twinkle, twinkle little star . . ."

A being such as Santa would never come to this barren icy rock, he thought but said nothing, not wanting to discourage his precious sunshine. He never wanted to see the smile fade from her adorable face.

A glowing streak flashed across the sky. Jessie gasped

and pointed. "Look, a falling star. Quick, make a wish!" She screwed her eyes shut. Her soft pink lips silently moved as she made her request to the heavens above.

"I cannot, for my wish would bring ruin upon the world."

This place had been his prison for what seemed like eons now. Jessie's parents worshiped and despised him as their dark god. Taking him prisoner had made them fabulously wealthy, but it also came with a high price. It was their eternal mission to hold him at bay from destroying them and, in turn, stop the chaos he would unleash unto the world. He knew Jessie's father secretly engaged in an elaborate system of human trafficking to sacrifice so many people to his bloodlust.

A snowball struck his shoulder, jarring him from his ruminations. Her playfulness kept his thoughts from drifting to dark and dangerous places. Jessie ran through the field, laughing wildly. Her lyrical lilt was sweet music to his ears. He silently stalked through the brush like a panther, fighting against his predatory urges to hunt her like easy prey as she hopped from bush to bush like a fleeing rabbit. Snowflakes drifted gently down, landing all over his pristine suit. He had no body heat to melt them, so the unique matrix of each tiny ice crystal glistened against the dark fabric. Another snowball struck his chest, spraying icy powder all over his overcoat. Giggling came from behind a thick fir tree.

"Got you good!"

The snow crunched beneath her boots as she ran away. The rainbow hues of the aurora borealis danced in the heavens above. In the northern lands, the native people believed the souls of the dead resided there. How many of those shimmering lights were the spirits of his victims gazing down upon him, angry for ending their all too short lives? If he ever passed from this world, would he also shine bright and eternal in the sky? He sighed, knowing such ideas were fanciful nonsense. He'd lived a sinful life. His soul was damned to suffer a far worse fate in the afterlife.

He shook off the melancholic thoughts and sped forth, feet barely touching the surface, leaving just a light dusting of his presence on the snow's virgin blanket. He again fought his instincts to attack the girl and sink his fangs into her tiny neck as she ran ahead of him, laughing excitedly. The blood of the innocent was always the most delicious, satiating his hunger like no other. Since the beginning of his imprisonment, he'd dreamed of hunting down the Harcourt family members one by one, hearing their screams shatter the night. But he refused to harm the sunshine that brought such splendid light into his eternal existence.

Jessie leaped onto a sled and pushed off the crest of a hill, speeding down the snowy slope with reckless abandon. Leaning side to side, she deftly steered around rocks and bushes. Exuberant squeals of delight filled the night air as she raced towards the bottom.

The dark figure leaped high into the air, his black overcoat flapping noisily in the breeze. All he could see for miles around was endless snow and ice. He landed gently beside her as the sled slowed to a stop.

The gables of the Harcourt manor house peeked over the bare tree top branches. She grabbed his hand with her soft purple mittens, leading him through the frozen estate grounds. The fountains were still, and the bushes and trees nothing but stark skeletons. All life here had retreated under the heavy blanket of winter. It was barren and cold, like him. He longed to see it in the spring when the gardens came to life again. But by then, the day's light lasted twenty-four hours, leaving him sleeping in his tomb until the arrival of the Arctic winter and its nearly endless darkness. When he emerged after his long spring sleep, he was weak and emaciated from the lengthy hibernation, deprived of his precious life-sustaining blood. The Harcourt family provided him with lost and forlorn men and women, chained outside his crypt awaiting their doom. He spattered the snow red with their essence.

The stately home of grey-stone bricks was built to harmonize with its surrounding. Soft light from arched bay windows gave the snow before the manor house a faint glow in the darkness. The colorful trappings of the holidays adorned the great room. White lights twinkled on the Tanenbaum, taking his thoughts back to Prussia in the sixteenth century. Christians decorated fir trees with colorful ornaments and candles during the winter solstice, glowing fiercely in the cold Germanic nights. The displays so enchanted him that he gave the villagers the gift of waiting until after the Christmas celebrations before he slaughtered them. Such beautiful carnage.

Jessie ran to the entrance and grabbed the knob with both hands, twisting until the door swung inward. She carefully stepped over the line of sea salt on the threshold. It wasn't there to melt the snow but rather as a ward preventing unclean souls, like himself, from entering the manor. That simple little line was all that kept him from entering and killing Jessie's father, freeing him to wreak havoc upon the world.

The girl stomped her feet in the mudroom, leaving slushy snow all over the marble flooring. She stripped off her boots and puffy parka, laying them on a wooden bench. Behind her stood the massive stone hearth decorated with evergreens. Smoldering grey logs glowed bright red within.

An elaborately carved grandfather clock chimed twelve times, ringing in Christmas day.

A smile crept onto his pale lips as the memory of her birth drifted into his mind. He'd seen many generations of Harcourt children grow up in the manor, but all had despised him as was proper. They lived in constant terror of him, but Jessie came into the world bold and fierce, born at home during the early winter. Her tiny cries escaped her parents' window at the eleventh hour. She was a child born into the night, just like him. He'd watched her grow from afar, seeing her mother lovingly cradle her near the window as a babe. When she was a toddler, Jessie placed her tiny finger against the frost-covered glass drawing silly faces to amuse the darkness.

He hadn't intended it, but he was the siren song that beckoned to her light from the lonely din of the arctic twilight. The girl was fearless in the night and often made these forays into the darkness to seek him out.

Jessie reached into a jar and pulled out a red and white candy cane, holding it out in offering. "Here, have this. These are my favorite."

The colors reminded him of blood-splattered snow. "I cannot, child."

"Why?"

"I do not eat candy." Still, he wondered about the flavor of it. The memories of what real food tasted like were long forgotten. The coppery tang of blood was the only thing he craved.

"Why?"

"Enough of these questions. You would not like the answers." He focused again on the colorful decorations that so delighted him.

Jessie replaced the candy cane in the jar and turned towards him. "Why don't ya come in?"

He tore his eyes away from the manor's festive display and looked down at her. The chapped redness was fading from her cheeks now that she was warming up.

"I can only enter with permission of the master of the manor, and you know your father will never invite me in."

Jessie shrugged. Her daddy was so mean for not letting Mr. Syn inside. It wasn't nice to leave him out in the cold all the time.

"Well, when I'm the lord of the manor, I'll let you in anytime you want. We can celebrate Christmas together, and my birthday . . . we'll be like Beauty and the Beast, dancing in the ballroom." She twirled around with her arms out wide.

"That would not be wise, dear child, and do not refer to yourself as a beast. You are not ugly enough for that."

She stopped her spinning and tilted her head at him, giggling. "You're silly. Why don't ya want to come and celebrate with me, be part of our family? We can open presents together," she said, swinging her arms back and forth.

"Because I am a monster. The Harcourt's are my keepers. We are not family and cannot be close in that way. I must keep my distance, or I will destroy all of humanity if I'm able to escape my imprisonment here."

"You won't hurt me. You're my friend." Jessie looked down at her wiggling toes.

Friend, the forbidden word that should have never been spoken. Most children feared the monster under their bed, Jessie wanted to befriend him. It nearly melted his cold, dead heart. No one had ever said that word to him before. He closed his eyes and released a heavy sigh. This was wrong. It was not in his nature to return her friendship. She was only a cheerful distraction in his endless existence.

"But I will. It's what monsters do." He wanted to warn her away. She was becoming too familiar with him. The girl should have no sympathy for him. It was dangerous for her not to see him as the vicious killer he was, lusting for blood and destruction. But the light of her being drew him like a moth to the flame. One day, she would be his keeper. It would be a heavy mantle for her to bear. She needed to feel detached from him to properly fulfill the role she was destined for.

Jessie's mouth opened in a wide yawn, revealing her missing front teeth. Her brown eyes were half-lidded as she looked down at the salt lining the threshold. She slid her pink sock-foot towards the fine white grains.

His eyes widened, alarmed, realizing what she was attempting. "Jessie, don't!" he yelled as her big toe moved within a half-inch of the line.

His harsh admonishment startled her, and she jumped back. "But why?" She stomped her foot in a huff.

He shook his head. The girl was recklessly defiant.

"For your safety. No more protests. You might wake your parents, and they will be very cross with you if they find out about your late-night expedition." He gently pushed his will on her young mind. "It's time for you to sleep now, my sunshine. Santa will not come to your home while you're still awake. Go to bed. Sweet dreams, little one."

This was a dangerous game she was playing. Jessie was too young to understand the consequences of her actions.

"Okay," she mumbled, gazing at him with glassy, unfocused eyes. "Night, night, Mr. Syn. Merry Christmas." She gave him a chubby-fingered wave and pushed the door closed. The lock turned and clicked softly. The precious girl was now secure with her family.

As he sped away into the dim evening, he looked back at the glow of the great room. He should disappear into the night and never see her again. Why can there be no darkness without light? Here in the arctic, they battled for control. The sun ruled during the summer, but darkness reigned in the winter. Jessie was like a candle shining brightly in a blackened window, a beacon welcoming him to the glow of the living. The battle between light and dark, an eternal struggle, so much like his inner conflict to destroy all those around him or keep his control so humanity remained safe. How can the light so beckon to the darkness?

For now, he was resolved to allow his imprisonment to continue to keep his beloved sunshine from harm. The Harcourts would celebrate the holiday in peace. If he was ever freed from this icy rock, he vowed to kill Jessie last—his gift to her on this celebration of Christ's birth.

MERRY CHRISTMAS, HANDSOME
JOSSLYN DYER

It had been a day. Janine Lamont sat on a bench in front of Burlington's country club, her head in her hands. The events of the last twenty-four hours played on repeat, though her mind remained foggy on the details. She remembered waking up in her apartment, drinking the requisite cup of black coffee, and logging onto her social media account. That's when things became complicated.

It didn't have to be this way. There were other options. But Scott was a bonehead and Janine didn't have a choice. She ripped a piece of torn fabric from her sleeve and examined it. No, she didn't have a choice. Scott made that choice for both of them. And now she had to pick up the pieces.

Janine rocked on the bench humming a tune, as if trying to ward off evil thoughts. She crumpled the piece of fabric, laughed, and threw it on the ground. "Merry Christmas indeed."

A passerby stopped and stared as Janine continued to hum. "Are you okay, miss?"

"I'm more than okay. It's Christmas. And I received the best gift."

"Are you aware of the circumstances? I mean, you do know what happened in the county club this evening, right?"

Janine cackled. "A Christmas wedding I suppose. Joyous occasion, huh?" She stood and twirled, her white dress flowing in the night breeze. "We wish you a merry Christmas, we wish you a merry Christmas. Where's your Christmas spirit?"

"I'll send a paramedic over right away. Whatever happened tonight, you're obviously a victim as well." The stranger rushed toward the entrance, leaving Janine alone once more.

"People don't know how to show holiday cheer anymore. It's a holiday people! Sing, dance, celebrate!" Janine twirled once more, tripped on the curb and fell face first on the ground.

J anine stretched and sat up in bed. Saturday. Two days until Christmas, her favorite holiday. She pushed aside the covers and slid into her slippers. Janine couldn't wait to begin her Saturday Christmas shopping trip with her best friend, Renice. Shopping, hot cocoa and sugar cookies had been their tradition since high school. And it was the most anticipated event of the year.

The small one-bedroom apartment worked for Janine. She maximized the space, using the kitchen peninsula as a desk for a makeshift office. She poured herself a cup of coffee and settled into the bar stool, logging onto her iPad and pulling up her social media account.

A knock on the door startled her as coffee spilled onto the keyboard. "Crap." Janine grabbed a paper towel as she yelled. "Come in!"

Renice breezed into the apartment, her face flush and as red as her hair. "You're not dressed. I hoped we could grab breakfast at that new pancake house."

Janine threw away the paper towel and grabbed her cup. "It won't take me long. Let me finish my coffee first."

"Well, hurry. I'm excited."

"You're cold too. Is it snowing out there or something?"

"I wish. Just hurry up."

Janine glanced at her iPad. Her social media account loaded on the screen. It was him. Her handsome. At least he had been. She couldn't claim him anymore. "So, pancake house and then the mall?"

"That's the plan."

Janine scrolled through her page and sighed. It had been a year since they last talked. A year since he had unfollowed all her accounts. But he hadn't blocked her. She wasn't sure if that was a good thing or a dangerous thing. "Cool."

"What are you looking at?"

Janine placed her coffee cup in the sink. "Nothing."

"Nothing? Then close it and get dressed."

"I just ... I have to ..."

Renice sighed and rolled her eyes. "Can't that wait?"

"Scott."

"What?"

"Scott. He posted new pictures."

"Are you still following him? Why torture yourself? I swear, you wouldn't function without me to save you from yourself."

Renice was her self-appointed bodyguard. A savior of

sorts. But even Renice couldn't save her from this. Janine fingered the screen, a tear welling in her eye. A picture of Scott with another woman. Scott smiling. The woman showing off a diamond ring. A picture of Scott wearing tux. The words *Getting married today at the country club* under the pictures. Her Scott. No, not Janine's anymore. He belonged to this other woman now. Janine turned off her iPad. "I'll be quick."

"Miss! Miss! Are you okay?"

Janine stirred as a husky voice spoke urgently in her ear. She lifted her head and stared at the hunky paramedic. *Stop. This isn't the time.* Pulling herself into a sitting position, she brushed the bits of debris and sidewalk cement from her face. "What happened?"

"Was hoping you could tell me. We responded to the event inside the building, but when I came out for more supplies, I found you face down on the sidewalk. Can you tell me what you saw?"

I saw my heart torn out and stomped on. Janine pushed herself onto her feet. "I didn't see anything."

"So, he came and hit you from behind? Coward. Based on the scene inside I'd have thought he'd of been more direct."

"Sorry, I can't help you." Janine trudged toward the bench and plopped down.

"Can I get you a ride home? This isn't the place for a young lady. Not after ..."

Janine waved him off laid down on the bench. She needed sleep, not babbling from young sexist paramedic.

"Where are we going? The pancake house is in the other direction. So is the mall."

"Yep."

"What's going on? You've been acting strange since you saw those pictures of Scott. What were they anyway?"

Janine white-knuckled the steering wheel. A knot grew in her stomach, full of despair and rage. Part of her wanted to cry. Part of her wanted to give Scott a tongue lashing. She had been his beautiful and he, her handsome. And now? How dare he get engaged and married so soon after their breakup? And without a word to her. Who did he think he was? They never discussed the reasons for their split. They never resolved their differences or explained their side of things. He just walked away, met someone else—someone Janine knew was just as neurotic—and never spoke to Janine again.

"Nothing. Pictures of Scott. Normal everyday pictures."

"Normal everyday pictures don't make you drive like a crazy person. You're going eighty in a thirty."

She had been speeding. How else would she get there on time? According to Scott's post, the wedding was at the country club in thirty minutes. That didn't leave enough time to ...

"Janine, tell me what's going on." Renice's face turned serious.

Telling Renice would be the proper thing to do. After all, they had been friends for years. If she couldn't tell her best friend, who could she tell? Janine drew in a breath. "The pictures. Scott met someone else."

"Yeah, we know that. And it happens. You broke up a year ago."

"He's getting married."

"Oh, Janine! I'm so sorry, honey." Renice placed a hand on her shoulder. "That must have been shocking."

"That's a word."

"If you want to reschedule, we don't have to go shopping today. We can go to my place, eat chocolate and watch sappy movies?"

A girls' afternoon, like in high school whenever a stupid boy dumped them. It sounded tempting. Janine's face softened. "80s movies marathon?"

"Anything you want."

That did sound better than the alternative. After all, barging into a wedding and demanding an audience with the groom only worked in movies. Janine loosened her grip on the steering wheel and turned onto the next street. Renice's apartment was the safer option. She would get through this, somehow.

"The killer left a clue."

Janine pulled herself up and sat on the bench, trying to make out the voices. Shadowed figures stood a few feet from the entrance, close enough to eavesdrop without detection.

A man in a suit approached the police officer and examined the Ziploc bag in her hands. "I hoped you had found the murder weapon. But at least this could have prints."

"More than that. It's a letter. A manifesto."

"Prints and a motive? Nice."

They found it. The piece of evidence that explained the past few hours. Janine stood and staggered toward the pair.

That piece of paper could explain what had happened to her the past few hours as well.

"Hey!" Janine faced the man. "Can I see that?"

He took a step back and held the bag close to his chest. "This is official evidence of the police department. Please step back, Ma'am."

Janine raised a shaky hand to her face and swiped back a lock of hair. "Ma'am? Do I look like a Ma'am?"

"Do you need assistance? Perhaps we can offer you a ride home."

"I need that letter. I need to know what happened."

"Were you at the wedding? Friends of the deceased?"

The police officer cupped a hand to her mouth. "Trauma, sir. She's clearly traumatized by the situation. Perhaps a visit with our counselor?"

"A therapist? I've had enough therapy the past year. Give me that letter. That's all I need." Janine lunged at the man.

"Get off." He pushed back against her as the police officer grabbed her shoulders.

"You don't understand. I need that letter. I need to know what happened the last few hours."

The three struggled on the sidewalk, pushing, pulling and screaming. Janine, still not feeling herself, kneed the man in his groin and head butted the police officer. She grabbed the plastic bag and ran back to the bench. Standing, she snatched the paper out of the bag and cleared her throat. "Are you curious about what happened? I know I am. This letter explains what seems to be a disturbing scene inside the country club. Is it really that bad? I haven't seen it. Oh well. Gather around and listen to the killer's manifesto as these officer's want to call it."

Janine opened her mouth when a single word silenced her.

"Enough."

Janine pulled into the parking lot. A girls' day would work. She could let out all her hurt, anger and angst on chocolate, 80s movies and her best friend. Renice could take the blow. After all, she hated Scott from the moment Janine started dating him. Renice had dubbed the date they broke up as Janine's Freedom Day, to be celebrated each year until Janine found someone worthy. That hadn't happened. Yet.

"You should feel sorry for that girl," Renice said.

"Sorry? She gets the fancy wedding, the presents, the honeymoon."

"Yeah. But she also gets to put up with Scott's sarcastic smart ass for the rest of her life. You dodged that one."

"Did I? What is he was the one and I let him get away?"

Renice laughed. "Really? How does he go from dickweed to the love of your life? First you want to kill him and then you want to smother him with affection. You're confusing yourself. And me."

Renice spoke truth. Scott always had an uncanny control over Janine. Even when she admitted he was toxic, she still couldn't leave him alone. And her obsessive and sometimes cruel behavior only served to push him farther away. Why couldn't she forget him?

"I'm so afraid of being wrong. What if I passed up the best guy out there? I pushed him away because of my crazy insecurities and some other girl snatched him up. Now I have to live with that. Live with my mistake."

"The mistake was dating him in the first place. You know that. Come on. Some wine, chocolate and movies will help." Renice hopped out of the car and closed the door.

Thoughts of Scott and their relationship ran through Janine's mind. His compliments, kindness and attention mixed with his lack of communication, guilt trips and massive ego. Janine spent just as much in tears as she did in ecstasy. Her mental health improved after the breakup. Her emotions leveled and her life seemed normal. At least Renice had commented on that fact. She did pity that girl. Especially since she didn't know what lay ahead of her.

Renice tapped on the window. "Are you coming?"

Staring at her friend while memories of Scott flashed in her mind, something snapped. Janine put the car in reverse, turned and sped toward the entrance. She had to know. Before Scott married, she had to know if breaking up had been a mistake.

Police officers surrounded Janine; their guns drawn. But that didn't faze her. They didn't want their main piece of evidence contaminated. Well, not more than Janine had already done. If they meant to coerce or intimidate, they chose the wrong person on the wrong day. Something happened in the country club. Something went wrong at Scott's wedding. And somehow Janine played a part. How else did she end up a bedraggled mess with torn clothes? Did she try to fend off the attacker? She had to know. Janine stared at the lone friendly face in front of her. Except it didn't seem so friendly.

"Enough."

"I don't think it's nearly enough. Not yet. It's nice of you to come, Renice. Always looking out for my wellbeing."

"Janine, give them the bag. And the letter."

She glanced at the letter and then at Renice. Her request would be the logical thing, perhaps the safest thing. "No."

"Janine. There's been enough hurt today. Get down and give them what they want."

"What they want? How about what I want? Did you ever think of that? No, you didn't. The entire time Scott and I dated, you said you supported me. But you didn't. You wanted things your way. Me and you. Scott came in between us, at least that's what you thought."

"Stop. I'm your best friend. Of course I have your best intentions at heart. I want you to be happy. And if Scott made you happy, I would have supported that. He didn't."

"He did. When we broke up, a part of me broke too. But you didn't see that."

"Therapy, Janine. You needed more therapy."

"Why? So I can get my head stuffed with things you wanted me to believe?"

"Because you aren't mentally balanced. It's my fault everything happened. I should have been driving. I shouldn't have gotten out of the car until you did. I should have known."

"Known what?"

Renice nodded at Janine's dress, splattered with red stains. "It's all over you."

The paper fell as Janine rubbed her fingers on the stains. Loud voices rang in her ears. Frightened faces, screams, crying played on her mind as she remembered the last few hours. No. She hiked up her dress and ran into the country club, pushing officers aside.

Christmas trees with red lights, tinsel and ribbon adorned the corners of the room. Tables set for a reception dotted the floor. Janine scooted through toward the dance floor. Scott and his wife had been dancing. It was their first dance. The dance Janine should have had. But it wasn't to be. Instead this girl, this stranger, had Scott's last name, his heart, and the wedding of Janine's dreams.

They smiled and kissed as the photographer snapped pictures. A crowd gathered, watching the happy couple. It all flooded back. Janine felt a sharp object stuffed into her boots. She reached and brandished the silver knife.

The dance floor, once a shade of walnut, flowed with red. Two bodies lay intertwined. Janine kneeled, tears streaking her face. She glanced at the knife, sticky with blood. She had done this. She had killed her true love and his bitch wife. She shook uncontrollably, piecing the events together.

"Why didn't you stop me?" Janine leveled her gaze with Renice. "If you knew I was unbalanced, if you knew I was coming here, why didn't you stop me?"

"I could never stop you. Even when you broke up, Scott had a bigger imprint on your life. It was always him, wasn't it? All those times I wanted to protect you from yourself? I wanted you for myself. But you never noticed. I wasn't good enough because I wasn't Scott. Well, now you can be united with him, ungrateful bitch." Renice raised a pistol and shot Janine in the chest. She crumpled over Scott's body as the letter fell to the ground.

Merry Christmas, Handsome. Shakespeare had it right all along: Love will kill you in the end.

REINDEER GAMES

GERRI R. GRAY

Faith stared at the colorful lights strung on the drooping spruce that stood in the corner of the isolated cabin, sap slowly bleeding from its axed trunk. Here it was, Christmas Eve. She had already ripped open her flesh-covered gift, and now, as usual, every inch of her body ached with boredom. "She didn't put up much of a fight, did she?" she said, almost in a yawn. "Not like the two before her. It was almost as if that bitch wanted us to torture and kill her. Some Christmas present."

She lit up a Marlboro and returned her gaze to the string of tiny bulbs, filling her eyes with flashings of green, yellow, blue, and her favorite color: red.

Outside, a light snow had begun to fall upon the mountains, turning white the bright crimson path of bloodstained snow leading from the cabin to the secluded spot in the dense of the forest where Faith's boyfriend, Wayne, had dumped the butchered body of the young woman he called 'the plaything.' That's what he liked to call the women whose lives he took great pleasure in snuffing out: playthings. They had no names, no identities, no relevance or importance. He regarded them as less than human. They were simply playthings to him, existing only to satisfy his brutal and demented desires.

Oblivious to the fevered, baleful barking of a hound that sprung up from somewhere in the near distance, Wayne wrapped his bloodstained hand around the bottle of Jack Daniel's that sat on the counter next to the sink, poured some whiskey into a shot glass, and downed it in one gulp. "The next one will be better, Faith," he promised. "Wait until you see the games I've got planned for her." He drifted into an almost trance-like state, enraptured in dark fantasy, as the frantic fit of barking turned into a single yelp, which silence quickly devoured.

Nuzzling the back of her head into her pillow, Faith shut her eyes and remembered a time, not very long ago, when Wayne was enraptured by her and her alone. But when his brutal undertakings with his female victims graduated to a sexual level, all of that seemed to change. When confronting Wayne about it, his reaction was one of anger and he threatened that she would 'meet the same fate as the others' if she ever attempted to leave him.

Having complete control and domination over others, including his partner in crime, was of the utmost importance to Wayne. He was the one in charge, and he intended for it to remain that way. There was no way he would ever permit any woman to manipulate him or stand in the way of his sexual gratification.

Faith opened her eyes and stared up at the wooden beams running across the ceiling. The steady rhythm of Wayne's raspy breathing danced in her ears, lulling as well as repulsing her, and she felt her eyelids grow heavy and droop like the branches of the dying tree in the corner. The car ride from the city to the cabin had been a long and tiresome one, which was now beginning to catch up to her, not to mention the letdown of a less-than-exciting kill. Time seemed to crawl to a stop as she surrendered to the encroaching drowsiness.

Her delicate, creamy features took on an almost angelic appearance as she slept. One might even use the word innocent if one didn't know any better. However, no visions of sugarplums danced in her head—only brutal scenes of torture and murder most savage.

There suddenly came a loud thump at the cabin's door. It was followed by another loud thump and what sounded like a sharp object scraping against the wood.

The bedsprings creaked as Faith bolted into a sitting position, a startled look on her face. "What was that?"

With his muscles tensed, Wayne picked up the knife he had used to disembowel the plaything. "It sure as hell ain't Santa Claus," he replied, his voice low. He made his way over to the window at the front of the cabin and peered out into the snowy remains of the afternoon. After a few moments, the bloodlust in his eyes subsided and he shut the curtain.

"There's nothing out there. Whatever it was, it's gone now."

He slithered into the creaking bed and gently ran the tip of the knife across Faith's throat, sliding it down to her cleavage and across her left breast, where is teasingly circled her engorged nipple. The chill of the steel brought a shudder of excitement to the naked girl and she shut her eyes and moaned, arousal building in her loins.

Faith was born with killer looks...and killer instincts. She knew Wayne regarded himself to be her mentor; however, her appetite for murder was roused long before he came into her life. She committed her first killing at the tender age of six when she crept up to her baby brother's crib in the dead of night and quietly smothered the life out of his tiny body with a pillow. The death was attributed to sudden infant death syndrome, and no one was ever the wiser. Her parents never once suspected that their sweet little girl with the rose-colored cheeks and ribboned pigtails could be a psychopath. She was sugar and spice and everything deadly.

Another thump, louder and more violent than the previous ones, sounded at the door, obliterating the couple's excitement. Like before, it was followed by an ominous scraping sound. Another thump came, and then another, and another.

Faith gave a gasp as her eyes widened with fear. An icy chill sprouted a multitude of goosebumps on the flesh of her forearms. She pulled the blanket up to her chin in a futile effort to warm herself.

"Wayne," she spoke in a near whisper. "You don't think that girl..."

"Don't talk like a fool," Wayne snapped as he vacated the bed and proceeded to the door, the knife clutched tightly in his hand. "I gutted that whore like a fish after you suffocated her with that plastic bag. Trust me on this; she's a slab of lifeless meat. She isn't going to come back from the dead and pound on the goddamn door like some kind of flesh-eating ghoul. This isn't *Night of the Living Dead*."

Faith held her breath and watched with eager attention as Wayne turned the knob and pulled the door open. A rush of cold air spilled into the cabin, ruffling Faith's tousled whorls of peroxide blonde and set tinkling the glass ornaments hanging from the boughs of the slowly dying Christmas tree.

And then her ears detected what sounded like a

hammer smacking a block of wood, and she felt her heart beating wildly as Wayne's fingers clawed at the crossbow quarrel protruding from his throat. She gasped as her malevolent swain stumbled backward and fell to the floor, blood spurting from his open mouth and a ghastly choking sound gurgling in his throat. His head cocked to one side, and he stared at the astounded girl, the life dimming in his eyes.

The sound of snow crunching under feet fractured the wintry silence, growing louder as each footstep drew nearer to the open door of the cabin. A man in a snow-crusted, camouflage hunting jacket appeared in the doorway, a crossbow in his gloved hand. He gazed down at Wayne's twitching body for a few moments, amused, before his eyes met Faith's. He emitted a deviant snicker and grinned, revealing four upper anterior teeth capped with gold crowns. The words "Merry Christmas" rolled off his tongue.

Faith bolted from the bed and rushed over to the man in the doorway. She threw her arms around him and joyously exclaimed, "Nick! I was starting to think you weren't going to show up!"

The grinning man embraced Faith, the crossbow still in his hand. "You know me better than that, angel. Have I ever let you down before?"

Faith giggled like a prepubescent girl and shook her head from side to side. She then disengaged from the hug and shut the door, her exposed body eager for the softly crackling logs in the fireplace to ward off the chill that had crept into the cabin. She paused to marvel at the puddle of blood slowly spreading out from underneath Wayne's speared neck, finding it rather amusing how the bright red color matched that of the glass ornaments on the tree. A smile tugged at her lips. This was turning out to be a very special Christmas Eve indeed.

"Get yourself dressed and then we'll haul this useless carcass out back to the woodshed." Nick winked one of his brown eyes. "I'll let you give him the first blow of the axe like I promised. That is, unless you've had second thoughts about doing it."

Faith experienced a perverse tingle race through her body as she threw on a heavy turtleneck sweater decorated with a reindeer and snowflakes.

"Are you kidding me? I've been dreaming of this day for almost a year! I can't wait to give that bastard the Lizzie Borden treatment. No one deserves to be hacked into little pieces more than he does!"

Nick laughed. "That's my girl." He looked down at Wayne. "Serial killing is an art, too exalted for a sloppy, rank amateur like him. To be a success in this business, you need to possess brains and cunning, as well as a lust for murder."

He shifted his gaze back to Faith, who was stepping into a pair of jeans with her back turned to him.

"Stick with me, and together we'll wreak havoc upon this stinking world while satisfying our darkest, most sadistic desires. Like a finely tuned killing machine, we'll rack up our victims in record-breaking numbers! You and me, angel—we'll be more famous than Fred and Rosemary West, Charles Starkweather and Caril Ann Fugate, Paul Bernardo and Karla Homolka, Ian Bradley and Myra Hindley..."

Faith was sitting on the edge of the bed and pulling on her boots when there came another loud thump at the door, followed by a scraping sound. The rosy glow in her cheeks paled, and her mouth dropped open.

Nick turned and stared at the door. "What the hell was that?"

"I don't know," replied Faith, a measure of uneasiness in her voice. "It happened a few times earlier, but I just assumed it was you trying to lure Wayne outside so you could..."

Another thump sounded, and Faith held her breath as Nick cautiously opened the door and looked around.

"Relax, angel. There's nothing out there but some hoof prints in the snow." Nick pointed down at the white ground. "Looks like they could be caribou tracks, but I'm no expert."

Faith looked puzzled. "Caribou?"

"Yeah. You know... a reindeer."

"Why on earth would an animal like that be trying to get inside the cabin? Is that something they normally do?"

Nick shrugged his shoulders. "Who knows what makes animals do the things they do? I wouldn't worry about it, though. Let's get this body out to the woodshed while there's still a bit of daylight left."

His hands latched onto Wayne's ankles and he began dragging the lifeless body out of the cabin, leaving a sticky snail-trail of smeared blood on the wooden floor.

Faith followed closely behind, taking care not to step on the slippery gore. Shutting the door behind her, she noticed it was riddled with gouges and deep slash marks. She stood motionless, her eyes transfixed on the scarred wood. A chill, like the icy fingertips of death, snaked its way down her body, and she turned the collar up on her coat.

"Come on, Lizzie Borden!" Nick shouted. "We've got work to do!"

Faith caught up with her lover and helped him drag Wayne through the snow to the back of the cabin.

Forgetting about the door, her thoughts turned to the butchering at hand. Anticipating the sight and sounds of the axe blade hacking Wayne's limbs from his torso made her breath quicken, and her loins began to tingle. There was no better aphrodisiac in this world for her than murder and mutilation.

Oh, how her creamy white hands ached to wrap themselves around the handle of the axe and plunge its heavy cutting head into Wayne's skull before dismembering him. Her tongue longed to taste the man's blood splattered on her lips. And the very idea that it would still be steaming with warmth ignited an even greater fire of excitement within her.

Nick opened the creaking door of the woodshed, and the sight of the waiting axe infused Faith with a peculiar urge to do unspeakable sexual things with Wayne's decapitated head. The taboo of it was titillating as well as disturbing to her, and it nearly brought her to an explosive orgasm right there on the spot.

Faith drew back with a start as Wayne's body suddenly gave a mighty heave. His eyes, glazed and empty like the glass orbs of a macabre doll, slowly rolled in their sockets until they were staring at hers. A terrible gurgling noise that sounded like 'you rotten bitch' bubbled up inside his bleeding throat.

"He's still alive!" Faith announced, worriedly.

Nick looked down at Wayne and grinned. "Just barely. But that'll make what we're going to do to him all the more fun! Just think how the look of terror in his eyes as he helplessly watches you raise the axe blade, anticipating that horrifying blow and his inevitable death, will feed your hunger for revenge."

A sudden clicking noise drew the attention of the killers

to the sight of a large reindeer standing about eight yards away, a massive thicket of antlers, like sharp blades, protruding from its head. From the corner of its foam-lathered mouth dangled a small, fleshy object. The animal's deep blue eyes stared strangely at Faith and Nick, causing a wave of uneasiness to ripple through their stomachs. All at once, it opened its mouth and emitted a loud, startling noise that sounded like a snort mixed with a bark, and upon doing so, dropped the fleshy object onto the pearly-white snow.

Faith gasped with shock as she realized what the reindeer had dropped was a woman's partially devoured hand, most likely belonging to Wayne's dead plaything out in the woods. "Oh, Jesus Christ!"

Nick looked stupefied. "Holy shit! That's the damnedest thing I've ever seen! I didn't know reindeers were carnivorous."

"They aren't," Faith replied. The sight of the hand in the snow captivated her eyes. "I remember back in school reading that they were herbivores. Their diet is supposed to consist of leaves and grass and other vegetation—not meat."

The reindeer snorted again and began to charge like a four-legged steam engine.

Nick grabbed Faith by the arm and quickly pulled her into the woodshed before slamming the door shut. The sound of feet dashing through the snow grew louder as the reindeer drew closer, and then there came a loud thud and the sound of splintering wood as its cloven hoofs smashed a hole in the door with violent force.

Faith let out a scream, and her body jolted as the reindeer backed up and snorted again as though preparing for another charge. Nick wrapped his hands around the axe, held it up in a position to strike, and waited with bated breath for the berserk beast to come smashing through the door. But instead, there came the sound of wild thrashing, accompanied by a gurgling cry, which endured for nearly ten seconds before sinking into a weak whimper. That soon gave way to a hellish symphony of ripping flesh and the crunching of bone.

Peering through the hole in the door, Faith and Nick watched with disbelieving eyes as the reindeer eviscerated Wayne's body before dragging it away into the snowy wilderness.

With a tone of urgency in his voice, Nick suggested to Faith that they hurry back to the safety of the cabin in case the "rabid" reindeer decided it would return. Faith nervously nodded her head in agreement, and the two psychopaths sprinted through the blood-soaked snow to the cabin. Faith opened the door and rushed inside with Nick trailing close behind, axe still in hand.

A bellowing scream shook Faith to the core, and she turned to catch sight of Nick rising up off the ground, his back impaled on the sharp antlers of another reindeer, considerably larger than the first one. With his arms flailing and his face contorted with pain, he was violently flung forward, his body landing halfway into the cabin.

Faith grabbed hold of his arms and pulled him all the way inside as the reindeer stood and watched from a few feet away. She quickly shut the door and locked it before attending to her injured lover. Lifting up his torn camouflage hunting jacket and the bloody, perforated shirt underneath it, she grimaced at the multiple puncture wounds on Nick's back. From one of them protruded part of a broken antler covered with blood and gristle.

"Don't worry, Nick," she reassured him, fighting the panic that was rising up inside her as his blood spilled out of his body. "You're going to be all right. I promise."

Nick screamed out in agony as Faith used her fingertips, without success, to extract the slippery piece of antler deeply imbedded in his back. "Jesus Christ! That God damned thing burns like a son of a bitch!"

After several fruitless attempts to remove the antler, Faith rushed to the kitchen and yanked a rusty metal toolbox from out of the cabinet under the sink. She threw it onto the countertop, opened the lid, and fumbled through its contents until she found a pair of pliers. At that moment, a rack of reindeer antlers smashed their way through the window above the sink, showering Faith with shards of broken glass. To her horror, the reindeer poked its head and neck all the way through the window, and its powerful jaws clamped down upon her left wrist, sending pain shooting down into her hand and up her arm. Screaming, she grabbed Wayne's bottle of whiskey from the counter with her other hand and swung it at the animal's snout with all her might, turning its nose red with blood and prompting it to release her wrist and retreat.

Ignoring her throbbing pain, Faith grabbed the pliers and several dishtowels and ran back to Nick, who was groaning in agony. Grasping the jagged end of the antler in the jaw of the pliers, she proceeded to extract the bony shaft with one long and steady pull. Nick screamed out like a madman as blood gushed from the unplugged wound and flowed down his sides and onto the floor, where it merged with Wayne's.

Faith then folded the dishtowels and applied them as a compress in an effort to arrest the spillage of blood from the wounds. However, Nick continued to bleed profusely. His face had gone pale and clammy, and he looked like he was slipping into shock.

"I can't get the bleeding to stop." Faith's attempt to mask

the distress in her voice and the dread in her eyes was futile. "I think it's best if I get you to a hospital, right away." Helping Nick to his feet, she added, "We'll take Wayne's pickup truck. It's not that far away. You can make it, baby. Just hang onto me for support."

With a biting wind whipping her face and stinging her cheeks with pellets of ice, Faith peered out from behind the cabin's partially opened door, hiding behind it like a shield. To her relief, not a single reindeer was in sight. She took Nick's arm and draped it around her shoulders. Together they trudged through the ankle-deep snow until they came to the pickup truck.

After helping Nick onto the passenger seat, Faith hurried around to the other side of the truck, climbed in, and started up the engine. Interwoven with static, Gene Autry's voice singing *Rudolph the Red-Nosed Reindeer* faded in and out on the radio. Faith immediately switched it off.

"Don't worry, baby. You're going to be all right," Faith promised her hemorrhaging passenger as she maneuvered the truck down the unplowed road that wound its way through the pine-mantled mountains.

All of a sudden, a pair of reindeer darted out from the trees lining the slippery, twisting road, their eyes reflecting the headlights of the pickup truck with an eerie, greenish glow. Faith jammed on the brakes and swerved to the right to avoid hitting them. The truck spun out of control and slid sideways into a tree with a loud thud. Both reindeer immediately began ramming the vehicle, puncturing all four of its tires with the spear-like tips of their antlers. Six other reindeer joined them—one of which leapt onto the steaming hood of the pickup and smashed out the windshield with its hoofs.

Covered with broken glass, Faith let out a blood-curdling scream as the reindeer bit down on Nick's arm and pulled him out of the truck and onto the hood. Faith fought with all her might to pull him back inside, but her strength proved to be no match for the power of the reindeer, and within a few terrifying moments, Nick was no longer in sight.

In an attempt to scare away the reindeer, Faith repeatedly blasted the horn, but to her horror, the herd gathered in a circle, surrounding the truck—watching and waiting. A bone-chilling wind was blowing snow into the cab through the missing windshield, and as the night grew darker, the temperature dropped.

What a way to spend Christmas Eve, Faith thought as she shivered from the cold.

Her breathing soon became shallow, and a wave of nausea surged over her. She stuck her head out the door to vomit, but all she could do was gag and dry heave. She then spotted the eight reindeer inching closer to the truck. She quickly shut the door and the herd immediately stopped in their tracks. Faith could feel all sixteen of their eyes boring into her—hungry, merciless, savoring every delicious morsel of her fear.

"Sooner or later, someone's got to come along and see that there's been an accident," Faith mumbled to herself, her words slightly slurred. "And then they'll send help and everything will be okay."

A loud snorting sound from one of the reindeer derailed Faith's train of thought.

"Nick?" she called out to the darkness. "Can you hear me? Are you out there? Nick! Please! Answer me! Nick!"

Faith listened for a reply, but her ears heard only the desolate wailing of the wind through the pine boughs. She tried her best to remain hopeful, but knew in her heart she would never hear Nick's voice again. Her instincts told her that he was dead, just like Wayne and the pretty little plaything that he had kidnapped and brought up to the cabin for slaughter.

As the minutes multiplied, a web of confusion enveloped Faith's mind, and she found herself drifting in and out of consciousness, her chills replaced by a strange and irrational sensation that her body was on fire. Succumbing to the final stages of hypothermia, she then slumped over onto the passenger seat, and her body gradually disappeared underneath a pearly white blanket of snow.

Christmas morning brought with it a cloudless sky of sapphire blue and brilliant sunshine that sparkled like diamonds on the snow-covered trees and ground.

Just as Faith had predicted, a passing motorist had spotted the wrecked pickup truck on the mountain road and called the police, who discovered Faith's corpse inside the snow-filled cab. She was frozen solid like a slab of venison in a meat freezer, and she was in death what she was in life—a cold-hearted bitch. Only now, her heart was far more colder...seventy degrees colder, to be exact.

CHRISTMAS SPIRIT
ALAINE GREYSON

Clara Evans dusted off her boots as she entered the barn. She loosened her scarf, allowing her long, auburn tresses to cascade down her back. Solitude. She longed for the privacy of her workshop, but was she alone? She scanned the barn, searching for evidence of another's presence. The woods contained magic and sorcery beyond what Clara could explain and kept her alert to mysterious forces.

She didn't have time to contend with nefarious beings tonight. The snow fell early this year and had already covered the ground between her cabin and the barn. The unexpected weather threw her off schedule but not for long. No matter how bad the weather got, she had deadlines to meet. Christmas was her busy season.

For the past ten years, Clara and her husband, Cedric, created handcrafted furniture for the town of Barrow, which lie five miles north of their cabin. While the work was in Barrow, they preferred the seclusion of the woods, with only the trees and animals to keep them company and the occasional wood sprite or fairy.

Their business flourished as Cedric's dining room tables and living room furniture grew in popularity. He was a master woodcrafter whose unique pieces put their competitors to shame.

Clara longed for human connection in town, but Cedric was comfortable with their simple way of life. No neighbors, no drama, and no nonsense made for a quiet existence. The only human contact they had was Damien Holt, Cedric's best friend.

She shrugged off her coat and scarf and angled herself in front of a custom-made chair. It was sturdy but missing the embellishments their clients had come to expect.

She eyed the top rail and tapped her finger on her nose. What design would suit this piece? She was an artist at heart and preferred to wait for inspiration. Cedric preferred to finish the piece and move on to the next.

"Flowers are always a good choice. Your pieces are piling up. Pick a design and get on with it." Cedric stretched out on the barn floor, his head on a bale of hay.

Clara startled. Cedric enjoyed appearing from nowhere and derailing her. She refocused and avoided his gaze. "There's something to be said for artistry. Patience was never your strong suit. It will get done in time." She snatched her chisel and put on her protective glasses. It would be a long night if Cedric planned on watching her. But she never could tell him what to do.

Clara concentrated on her chosen design—a sunrise that covered the top rail—and ignored Cedric's moans of disdain. She would meet their Christmas deadline, but she would do it her way. No one dictated her designs, not even her husband.

As she focused on the chair, the barn doors swung open. Damien's large frame entered and fixated on Clara. "It's fixing to storm tonight. These pieces can wait. Let's get to the house and warm up before it gets bad."

Clara expelled a sigh. So much for solitude. Between Cedric and Damien, she wouldn't accomplish much. Determined to finish her project, she refused to look in his direction and kept chiseling. "Storm or not, Christmas is in a week. I don't have much time."

Damien crossed his arms. "I'm not leaving you out here alone. It's too dangerous. I'm making an executive decision. When you're done with this chair, I'm escorting you to the house."

Clara shook her head and jerked it in Cedric's direction. "I'm not alone, Damien. Cedric is here. I'll be safe with him."

Damien paused and looked toward the hay bales. He gulped and sat on a pile of wooden planks. "Cedric. Of course. How silly of me."

Cedric chortled. "Silly indeed. Insinuating I can't look after my own wife. The audacity!"

Clara gave Cedric a warning glance then returned to her design. She wasn't in the mood to referee tonight. The two alpha males needed to sort their differences without her participation. She longed for the days when the three of them got along.

Damien surveyed the room and leaned toward Clara. "We need to talk. This past year has been a struggle."

"It's fine. We made it through. Only seven chairs and our orders will be complete. You can take a break after the holidays. You've earned it."

"It's not that, and you know it. I enjoy helping you keep the business going. I'm worried about you though."

Clara placed her chisel on the floor and faced Damien. He had saved their company when they had fallen behind on orders last winter. They wouldn't have survived without his expertise and hard work. Cedric refused to admit it, but Clara was grateful.

"You're a good friend. You stepped in when I needed you. But I'm fine." She squeezed his hands and smiled.

Cedric's eyes bulged. He rose from the hay bales and approached them. "Get your hands off my wife!"

The barn doors flung open, and a waft of cold air spread between them. Damien flinched and gathered his scarf around his face. "Snow's coming down harder now." He strode to the entrance and gazed as the snow danced in the moonlight.

Clara clenched her jaw and raised her gaze toward Cedric. "That was unnecessary. You owe Damien an apology. We wouldn't have finished our orders without his help."

Cedric lowered his gaze and retreated to the hay bales. He shot Damien a menacing grin as he settled onto the floor.

Clara strode to the barn doors and peered at the falling snow. "It's getting bad. We should head to the house."

"That's the wisest thing you've said. Is Cedric coming?"

Clara rubbed her necklace and gazed at her husband. "He always does."

The wind blew the snow sideways as Clara and Damien trudged to the house. Once again, Cedric overreacted to a simple gesture. Clara didn't understand why he was so possessive. Damien was his best friend and the only person outside of Clara whom he trusted. Why get upset because they briefly touched hands? They needed to discuss this so it didn't happen again. If Damien grew mad and walked away, they wouldn't be able to keep the business afloat. Clara made a mental note to talk with Cedric after Damien left.

The cabin stood amidst a myriad of evergreen and pine trees, shrouded by a canopy of green. Snow laid atop the branches, creating the ideal Christmas scene. Clara gazed at the full moon and hoped Cedric would behave tonight. She needed a decent night's sleep.

Damien opened the back door and stomped his boots on the ground. "Want me to put on a pot of hot chocolate before I go?"

"Thanks, but that's okay. I'm hoping to turn in early and catch up on some sleep. We have a busy day tomorrow."

Damien barreled through the house to the front door. "I better get going before I'm snowed in. The back roads are impassable when it snows."

Clara followed him to the front porch and watched as he dug out his truck. If any vehicle could navigate these roads in a snowstorm, it was Damien's truck. She fingered her necklace as she watched him shovel the snow that had piled around his tires. Hidden because of his heavy coat, but Clara knew the muscle-bound man inside of it. Damien had worked alongside Cedric since their teenage years, cutting down trees and fashioning furniture. His biceps were built for hard labor, and Clara noticed them every summer. Not that she was attracted. She had Cedric, after all. But it was hard to miss.

Not only was he built, but Damien was also the most generous man she knew. She didn't know why he was still single. If she had a female friend, she would have played matchmaker. But she had no one outside of the cabin. Damien deserved a happy ever after with someone.

A waft of air bristled her neck as she watched.

"Is he leaving?"

Clara closed her eyes and breathed deeply. "He's trying to, if the roads are passable. Would you be mad if he had to stay?"

"I know he's been a help to you, and I appreciate that, but he interferes. Is it wrong to want you for myself?"

Clara faced Cedric, her hands clenched at her side. "You have me, Cedric. I promised myself to you on our wedding day, and I won't renege on my vow. I just want to have Christmas, like before, with no drama. If Damien has to stay, can you help him feel at home?"

Cedric's face reddened. "It's my home, Clara. Not his. I won't let him feel comfortable here. I see the way he looks at you."

Clara glanced between the two and smirked. "Damien doesn't want me. He feels obligated to protect me because he loves you."

Cedric chortled. "His protection is not needed. I will watch over you. After this storm, we will cut ties."

Clara's eyes grew round. "You can't do that. I won't let you."

"Enough. I'll give you time to say your goodbyes." Cedric clunked into the house.

Clara rested her arms on the porch railing and stared. Damien wasn't in competition for her affection, was he? Why was Cedric jealous? At one point, the two men were inseparable, but now the divide threatened to tear everything Clara knew apart. If she could bridge the space between them, life would return to normal. At least she hoped.

Clara cupped her hands to her mouth. "Are you sure it's safe to drive?"

Damien turned in her direction, his face flush from the

cold. "It's pretty deep out here. It'll take some time, but I have chains if I need them."

"Why don't you stay the night? It'll be safer in the morning."

Damien leaned the shovel against the truck and trudged through the snow drift to the porch. "Would Cedric allow it?"

Clara clutched her necklace and leveled her gaze. "I allow it. Your safety is more important than his misplaced anger. Come inside and let me make you some hot chocolate. Extra marshmallows?"

Damien removed his hat and ran his fingers through his hair. "I'm going to regret this, but that sounds nice."

Clara gathered her courage as she led Damien into the living room. At Christmas, this was her favorite room. They had decorated the fireplace with garland and stockings. A six-foot Christmas tree stood in the corner, decorated with silver and blue ribbons and ornaments. The room used to bring her comfort, but now she entered with trepidation.

She panned the room. *Good. Cedric isn't here.* She hoped he would confine himself to their bedroom. "Make yourself comfortable. I'll prepare some hot chocolate and snacks."

Clara's gaze lingered on Damien as he yanked off his coat and scarf. His biceps bulged through his polo shirt—evidence of a life spent performing hard labor. He was an attractive man with a soul that matched. Her mouth hung open as he bent to place his belongings on the armchair. *Snap out of it, stupid. Cedric could be anywhere. Don't cause a scene because of your lust.* Clara shook thoughts of Damien from her head and plodded to the kitchen.

She retrieved a pot from the cabinet, filled it with milk and placed it on the stove to boil. Insisting Damien stay the night was the humane choice, even if it meant consequences with Cedric.

As she poured the hot chocolate mix into the pot, her arms bristled from a blast of cold air.

"You defied me."

Clara jolted. "It was necessary. Your ire isn't worth Damien's life. He'll leave as soon as the roads clear."

"That could be days. No one plows the roads back here. Damien is resourceful and would have found a way."

Clara faced Cedric. He leaned on the doorframe between the kitchen and the hallway, sporting a dissatisfied frown. Clara had hoped they would become closer out here, separated from the rest of humanity, but it only caused grief and strife. Cedric had changed from the man she'd married. But she was unwilling to push her loyalty and memories aside to admit the truth. Somehow the three of them would surpass this and hopefully emerge stronger.

"He's staying, and that's final. You can brood about it all you want, but you're not changing my mind. You have a choice. You can retreat to our bedroom for the duration, or you can join us for hot chocolate and Christmas cookies. Either way, please behave."

Cedric grunted and disappeared into the hallway.

Clara finished stirring the hot chocolate and arranged a tray for the living room. She wasn't sure what Cedric would decide, but she knew he wasn't happy. She girded herself for whatever awaited her.

"Hot chocolate and sugar cookies. The perfect treat for a snowy night." Damien scooped a cookie and nibbled. "Thank you for your hospitality. I hope my presence isn't creating difficulties with Cedric."

Clara waved her hand. "I can deal with my husband. I'm glad you're here and you're safe. That's all that matters."

"*Hmph.*"

Clara raised her gaze and saw Cedric standing in the corner, his arms folded. He had decided to join them. She wasn't sure if that was a victory or the beginning of defeat.

Damien angled his body toward Clara so their knees touched. The unexpected contact caused her heart to skip a beat. She didn't understand her physical reaction. Her heart belonged to Cedric, so why did her insides tingle at Damien's touch?

He grasped her hands and leveled his gaze with hers. "I meant it when I said I was worried. You're keeping the business afloat, but what about you. Are you okay? Eventually you have to deal with your feelings."

Clara took a deep breath and closed her eyes. "This isn't the time to talk about it. I appreciate your concern but—"

"Cedric. Clara, you can't pretend that last Christmas didn't happen. Things are different now. You have to process your feelings and move on."

Clara glanced toward the corner of the room. Was Damien aware Cedric was listening? She girded herself, prepared for his reaction.

Cedric's face reddened. He approached the couch, his shape increasing with his anger.

Clara outstretched a hand to stop him, but Cedric ignored her plea.

Damien jolted upright and screamed as a mug of hot chocolate covered his face and chest.

"I'm so sorry, Damien." Clara grabbed a towel and blotted his face. She shot Cedric a scowl and led Damien down the hallway. "A shower will help you feel better. Some of Cedric's clothes are in the hallway closet. You can borrow whatever you want." She turned around and marched back to the living room. "What was that about? You could have injured him!"

"He was interfering. All that talk about you moving on. He's trying to snag you for himself."

"Why would he do that? He knows I'm married to you. It makes no sense."

"You're gullible. What man wouldn't want you?" Cedric stood in front of her and traced the outline of her face. "You're the most beautiful woman I've ever met. The day we married was the best day of my life. I'm not letting someone take that from me."

"No one is taking anything from you, Cedric."

His hands moved to her neck as he caressed her sapphire necklace. "As long as you wear my necklace, we'll be together. It suits you, accentuates the golden specks in your eyes."

Clara sighed. This was the part of Cedric she missed. His soft, romantic side attracted her when they had met. From outward appearances, Cedric would intimidate anyone with his bulging biceps and six-pack abs. But his gentle spirit and unwavering love proved to be the attributes that had won her heart.

She rubbed the necklace and strode to the couch. "I made a vow, and I stand by it. To death do us part."

"Beyond death. My love for you spans time and human existence. That's why you must wear the necklace. It binds us together."

But can I continue to live like this? Clara tapped her fingers on her chest. There had to be a solution. She wanted Cedric *and* Damien in her life. She wasn't prepared to choose.

"I don't understand what changed. Damien and I have

been friends our entire marriage, and you didn't mind. But now you feel threatened."

Cedric moaned and sunk into the armchair.

Damien wandered into the room, drying his hair with a towel. Clara gaped at the bare-chested figure, making no attempt to hide it from Cedric.

"You can wear one of Cedric's shirts."

Damien tilted his head and smirked. "And risk his wrath? I'll pass."

Yet you think standing bear-chested in my living room won't anger him? Clara gathered her senses and eyed Cedric. He sat drumming his fingers on his knees and avoiding Damien's gaze.

"Can we talk without him hanging around?" Damien sat next to Clara and scanned the room.

Clara rubbed her necklace. "He gets angry when you touch me. Stay to your side of the couch." She scooted to the opposite side and cast Cedric a warning glance.

Damien leaned forward and tapped his thumbs. "It's been a year, Clara. I'm not expecting you to forget about him, but, at some point, you must let him go. He can't rest and you can't live if you're stuck in the past."

Clara gazed at Cedric. After ten years of marriage, how could she let him go? "I made a vow, Damien. You were there. I can't let him go because we belong together. Til death do us part."

Damien sighed. "You said death, Clara. Death do you part. I would say that criteria has been met."

A tear streaked Clara's face. "You want me to send him away? To where? How do I know he will rest? He's happy here, with me. I can't do it."

"If you don't, he will consume you. Living with a spirit is not a fulfilling life. It's time you started living for you."

Cedric contorted his face and mimicked Damien. "Don't listen to him. He's trying to scare you. What does he know about true love anyway?"

Clara stood and paced the room. Damien was right. Her vow didn't tie her to Cedric now, but love did. She couldn't send him away, not knowing where he would go.

"Cedric was my best friend. I loved him like a brother. He would want the best for you. And that's in the land of the living, not in the land of the dead."

"Keep talking, *brother*. Clara is my wife, and I know what's best for her." Cedric straightened himself and met Clara's gaze. "We are meant for each other, a mhuirnín. Don't be fooled by his manipulations."

Gaelic. Clara melted when he called her *darling* in Gaelic. He pulled out all the stops. But it still left her confused. What if Damien was right?

She scratched the back of her neck and fiddled with the clasp. If only she knew Cedric's destination in the afterlife, then she could let him rest. But she was his only tie to the mortal realm. Sending him away, losing him again, would destroy her.

"Why do you keep touching your necklace?" Damien approached her and caressed the blue stone. "When Cedric died last Christmas, this necklace appeared under the tree. Tell me about it, Clara."

The front door opened, and a blast of cold air invaded the space. Books flew off the shelf, joining with coffee mugs and ceramic pieces, causing a tornado. Damien tried to shield Clara, but the force knocked both onto the couch.

"Enough! I told you he would interfere. You belong to me, Clara, and I will make sure you never escape." Cedric blew a blast of cold air toward Damien, thrusting him out the front door.

Clara stood wide-eyed, Cedric's violent behavior shocking her. This wasn't the man she fell in love with or the man she had married. Her heart and her brain fought until thoughts of Damien in the freezing cold won out.

"What are you doing? This isn't right."

"Ah, but it is. We belong to each other, and no one can destroy our love." Cedric spun around as a mist crawled over the house. "Together, forever. Time stands still for us."

A fog surrounded the house, making it invisible to the outside world. Clara banged on the front door. There had to be a way out. Somehow, she had to save Damien. As the fog enveloped her, Clara fell to floor. How could she save Damien when she couldn't even save herself?

The mist carried Clara into the living room and laid her on the couch. "You're mine. You've always been mine. And now no one can tear us apart."

ONCE UPON A MOUSE

A. S. MACKENZIE

"This place is ..."

"Right?"

Harper turned in a small circle where she stood in the foyer, eyes big and bright, taking in the space.

"It's unbelievable," she said in barely a whisper. Dean didn't seem to notice as he quickly gathered their bags from the front porch and hastily brought them in to sit beside the door.

"The guy said that the furnace takes a bit to warm up, so unless we want to freeze tonight, we need to get it started," he called over his shoulder as he exited the door to grab the last of the bags.

"Hmmm?" she said as she absently moved to the opening between the foyer and the living room. Her hand reached out and rested on the polished wood that made up the opening, eyes still big and bright as her hand slid down its impossibly smooth surface.

Dean came back in with the last of their bags, set them down, and walked up to her, wrapping his arms around her from behind. She gave a small giggle as he picked her up and spun her around. He set her gently back down when she said, "That's enough," and moved around to stand in front of her.

"Well, what do you think?"

She said nothing for a moment as she looked around some more, her hands resting on his arms, her mouth moving to make words but nothing coming out. The smile she wore grew until she chuckled, looked him in the eyes, and said, "It's perfect."

"*Haha!*" He laughed in triumph and wrapped his arms around her again and gave her a kiss.

"Welcome home, Harps."

She reached up, put a hand on the side of his face, and replied, "Our home."

After a few more minutes, he said, "As much as I hate to do this, I need to go check the furnace and get it going. It's supposed to drop low tonight with snow, and I don't know about you, but I don't want to freeze to death two days before Christmas in our brand-new home."

She giggled, gave him a playful push, and said, "Well, get going! I'm certain I know a way to keep us warm, but maybe not that warm." She winked.

He pretended to stop frozen in mid-step and said with a mischievous grin, "Really? Want to put it to the test?"

"Get going!" she replied, giving him a push.

"Alright, but now we may never know." He rounded the corner behind the stairs to reach for the basement door.

She didn't reply but instead went to one of the bags they brought with them and pulled out a wreath and a door hanger. Taking it, she set it on the front of the door, smiled, and said "Merry Christmas to us" as she shut the door and grabbed a couple of their bags and took to the steps to find their room.

The staircase was made with dark, stained wood, and the window at the top was boarded over. It looked to have been completely broken at some point, and a section of plywood had been secured over it from the outside. While it offered protection from the growing cold and wind outside, it did nothing to let any light in, so the area was very dark. The light switch at the top of the stairs was one of the old fashioned, two-button styles so prevalent in the older homes of this type. She pressed the upper button and heard a click and a buzz, but no light turned on. Frowning slightly and looking around, she pressed the lower button. It clicked while the buzzing stopped.

"Great. Just what we need before the holiday: a wiring project."

She pressed the upper button again and again, hearing a click then a buzz. She leaned her ear towards the wall and listened as the buzz grew louder. A loud *click* made her jump. Then the buzzing stopped, and the light hanging above the landing started to glow, quickly gaining brightness.

"That was weird," she said, her frown deepening.

Taking advantage of the dimly lit space, she took the bags down the hall, stopping at the two open doors for the other bedrooms and clicking their light switches on. Neither room turned on or even made a buzz. The small bathroom did the same at first, but then the buzz started and the light flickered to life. Finally, she made it to the double doors at the end. Pushing them open, she was greeted by warm sunlight shining through the stained glass above the windows, giving the room a cozy, colorful, and almost ethereal look. Still, she hit the light switch, figuring she should check everywhere. None of the lights were particularly bright, and the buzzing was annoying.

The room faced over the front of the house and showed a view of the property through four large windows, each with their own stained glass displays above. Stepping forward, she looked out to see the rolling hills of their new property stretching before them, the trees made bare by the cold. It looked to her like images she'd seen as a child of creepy old manor houses in England where even the fountains were haunted.

She was so taken with the beauty of their newfound home that she didn't notice the movement at first. When it registered out of the corner of her eye, she gasped and spun to see three mice in the far corner of the room. They were small, like field mice, and gray with little round ears.

"No, no, no, no!" she exclaimed, stomping towards them to frighten them away. They scurried over to a small hole in the baseboard, where they ducked completely out of sight.

"Great ... more of what we need."

She set the bags on the floor and turned to head back down and grab more when she paused. Something in the stained glass caught her attention. Turning, she stepped closer to the four panels, head-cocked in concentration.

"That's a weird thing to put ..." she said, letting the words trail off.

One each of the four panels was a scene, she assumed, but not of anything she recognized. The first showed hills with hundreds of small dots. The second showed a house, similar to this one, with the dots all around. The third showed a mouse, in great detail, with sunlight shining through its ears. The fourth was mostly made of red glass, but again with the hundreds of dots.

Turning back to the hole in the baseboard, she could barely make out a small face with whiskers looking back at her.

A chill ran across her shoulders. She shook it off and chided herself for being so easy to frighten. Heading back down the hall, she paused to look into the other rooms. The movers had been here earlier that day and set all their belongings in these two rooms, along with another portion in the living space downstairs. She smiled despite the scene that just occurred in the bedroom, thinking now about how much she enjoyed unpacking. It was, to her, a therapeutic endeavor. Her husband didn't feel the same, but that was alright by her. She'd rather do it her way, anyway.

When she returned to their bags on the main floor, he was just coming back up the stairs from the basement. His face had a streak of soot across it to go along with the big grin he carried.

"Got it! That's an old beast down there that runs on oil. Once we can, we should replace that with something a bit more efficient. But for now, we will be toasty warm!"

"That's great," she said, then paused before picking up the next round of bags. "Dean, tell me again. How did you find this place?"

"You love to hear this story, huh?"

"Humor me," she replied, though the smile she wore was more forced than humorous. She didn't want to tell him about the wiring and the mice just yet. The stained-glass images flashed in her mind for a moment, too, before she pushed them aside.

"Okay, well, as you know, I was up here scouting a good location for our bakery. When I found that perfect spot next door to the coffee shop and the bookstore, I just thought this couldn't be any better. But when I went to sign the lease for the space, a guy was there from town who asked about us moving in. We got to talking, though he was kinda quiet and a little weird, and he asked where we were going to live. I said that was next on our plans, and he mentioned that he had a great aunt whose house was empty right now but that he'd be willing to let go of it to a good family.

"I don't know, I guess I impressed him somehow because he said he liked me and had a good feeling about us. He gave me the address, his phone number, and said to go check it out. I drove out here, saw the property and the house, got back in the car, and called him. The price he gave was so good, and you remember I called you right away and sent pics. When you agreed, well, the rest is history."

"Wait, so you didn't even come inside?"

He shook his head. "No, he didn't give me the key. I just walked around and looked through the windows. It looked great. Why? You having some buyer's remorse?"

She ramped up her grin and replied, "No, hon, of course not. It's just we may be taking on too much with the new store and this house. Gotta tell you, there are some wiring issues I've seen already, and—"

"Yeah, I saw the wiring downstairs," he interrupted. "It's the old fabric hook-and-loop kind. That should be one of the first things we tackle."

"Yes," she said with a tinge of annoyance, unhappy about being interrupted. "I was saying that. I've turned on the light switches in different parts of the house, and we aren't getting much light. Plus, I think there are transformers or something to handle the electricity because the lights buzz. But also, there are mice."

"Yeah, I kind figured there would be."

She couldn't hide the shock that crossed her face. "What? You knew there would be mice in our house?"

He raised his hands innocently. "No, hold on, I didn't know for sure. But this house is over a hundred years old. I'd be very surprised if there weren't mice in here, especially with all the grass and woods out there. We can get a cat if you want."

"A cat? A cat is your big plan? Just how many cats are we talking for what's likely going on here? Three? Four? Eight? Just how many cats do you think we will need to rid this place of all these mice?"

"Yeah ... Harps, you okay? You were so impressed with the place a few minutes ago and now you seem angry about it. What happened?"

Shaking her head and turning back to their things still by the door, Harper said, "No. No, I'm fine. Just a new place I guess and getting confronted with how not-idyllic it actually is. I'm fine." Taking two suitcases, she went past him and up the stairs. He said nothing but grabbed the last couple of bags and followed.

In the bedroom at the end of the hall, he set the luggage down next to the others and gave a long, low whistle as he looked out over the front of the property from the windows.

"Can you believe he let this place go for so cheap? Man, some people just don't know what they have."

She didn't reply but instead stood with her arms wrapped around herself, glancing down to the hole in the baseboard. Noticing her silence, Dean turned and saw her staring, then followed her gaze.

"What's that?" he asked. "Is that where you saw a mouse?"

"Three."

He paused. "Three? Huh ... don't normally see them in groups like that." He walked over to the hole, knelt, and peered in. It was just a couple of inches wide and tall, but he could just make out the space behind it and could see a little of the plasterboard that made of the wall space. But no mice.

"Well, tell you what. I'm going to go down to the kitchen and grab the aluminum foil from one of the boxes. I'll start here and shove some into there, then go room-by-room and put more in any other holes I find. Deal?"

"Aluminum foil?"

He nodded. "Yeah, my dad taught me that when I was a kid. Mice and rats don't like to chew on the stuff, so it makes a good barrier."

She gave a resigned shrug and said, "Go for it, I guess. Not much else we can do at the moment."

He stood and headed for the door, but she stopped him with a hand on his arm.

"Before you go, what do you make of the stained-glass up there?"

Looking past her, he scrunched his eyes to take in the bright images. The sun was low enough on the horizon that they were getting the full effect of the light. He studied them for a few moments and replied, "Weird ... guess whoever lived here before really liked mice? I don't know." Then he gave her a quick kiss on the cheek and left the room.

With another glance to the hole in the wall, she turned and exited. Deciding to take her mind off the whole mouse thing, she set herself the task of getting their bed ready for the night. Going through the moved items, she found all the pieces for their bed frame. Taking them into the room, she set them to the side and went back for the headboard. This time when she walked back in, she froze.

Standing on their luggage and the pieces of the bed frame were mice. Eight of them. All upright on their hindquarters, looking at her.

Not knowing exactly what to do, she just yelled for Dean.

"If you're coming with that foil, you better hurry!"

She couldn't tell if he had heard her or not, but she knew she needed to do something. Taking the headboard up a little higher she let it fall on to its legs and the wrought iron weight fell with a thump.

The mice took off as one, all heading to the hole in the wall. The last one paused and turned to look at her before it, too, ducked into the hole.

"Dean!"

She heard his footsteps on the stairs and then in the hall.

"What is it? Are you okay?" he asked, looking around the room to see what had caused her concern.

"There were more of them this time! Eight, Dean! Eight mice were on our things. I just set those things down, went and grabbed this headboard, and when I came in, they were everywhere in here."

"Honey, are you sure? Eight is a lot—"

"Yes! Don't patronize me! I know how to count to eight!"

"Fine, yes, okay, you saw eight. What happened to them?"

She took a big, calming breath in and said, "I dropped the headboard, and it made a loud enough noise to run them off. But Dean ... the weird thing is, I don't think they ran because they were scared. They all ran together, and I could swear ... No, you know what, that's silly. I'm just imagining things ..."

"Like eight mice?"

She turned and fixed him with an icy glare.

"Do not mock me. I meant I was imagining the last mouse stopping to look directly at me."

"Okay, yeah, I don't know what's going on," he retorted.

Lifting the roll of aluminum foil in his hand, he added, "But, why don't we just take care of this right now, and I'll check tomorrow if the hardware store is open, even though it's Christmas Eve, and pick up some mouse traps. Deal?"

Not saying anything, she waved her hand in a 'go ahead' gesture.

He set to work on gathering up a ball of foil and shoving it into the hole in the baseboard. Once he felt certain it covered the space well enough, he indicated that he was going to continue in the rest of the house.

Harper went back to assembling the bed frame, attaching the headboard, then the retrieved footboard. Once satisfied, she found the ideal spot on the wall which would give them the best view from their bed and set the entire frame in place. When she was struggling to move the box spring down the hall, she heard the faint sound of brakes squealing out front. Leaning the box frame against the wall of the hall, she went back into the large room and looked out the windows.

In their front drive area, a large box truck had arrived and was backing up to them. Two men got out of the cab once it stopped, opened the back rolling door, then hopped up to sit in the open space, their legs dangling over the fender. They seemed to be waiting for something.

Before she could call for Dean, a second truck arrived. This one an old model she recognized as the one belonging to the previous owner when they met this morning to sign for the keys. She wasn't expecting him or anyone else today, so she began to get a bit concerned that there was an issue with the sale.

"Dean? Dean, honey ... are you up here?"

He emerged from the bedroom closest to the stairs, foil roll still in hand.

"It's funny," he said as he walked towards her. "There is exactly one hole, the same size, in all these bedrooms and the bathroom. If I didn't know any better, I'd guess someone made ... the ... holes ..." His words trailed off as he came to stand beside her and looked out at the new arrivals.

"Who are they?" he asked.

"No idea, but isn't that the previous owner, Mr. Guster?"

"Yeah, what's he doing here, too?"

Dean handed the roll of aluminum foil to her and said, "I'll go find out."

He wasn't out of the room long before Mr. Guster exited his truck, walked around to the bed, and pulled out several large planks of wood. Gesturing to the two men, he motioned for them to join him as he walked to the front door. She heard their boots on the old wood of the porch and then heard knocking.

And more knocking. And even more.

"Hey!" Dean yelled from the stairs.

Turning, she raced down the hall and asked, "What's going on?"

"They're nailing something to the door!"

"What?" she yelled. It couldn't have been what she thought she heard.

Harper came down the stairs quick enough to see Dean run to the door and try to push it open. It wouldn't budge, so he threw his shoulder into it. With each impact, the wreath bounced on the door. The two men who had come with the truck weren't there anymore. Then she heard banging on the back door. As she turned to go check it out, she could see Mr. Guster standing on the other side of the door, his face passive.

"What the hell are you doing?!" Dean yelled, banging himself into the door repeatedly.

She ran to the back door just as the two men stepped back, their barricade seemingly in place. Still she tried the door and it, too, was immobile.

"Why?" she yelled at the men, who both shared the same expression as Mr. Guster.

Running back to Dean, she yelled, "The back door is shut, too! Dean, what's going on?!"

"I don't know," he hollered back. He stopped banging against the door long enough to stare at Mr. Guster. "What are you doing? This is our house now! Open this door!"

Without a hint of expression, Mr. Guster said, "This is their house. Always has been. Always will be. It just needs to be fed from time to time. It happens that now is that time."

"What? What needs to be fed? Listen, you crazy old man, when I get out of here, I'm going to sue the shit out of you and press all kinds of goddamn charges! You hear me? You're going to go to jail unless you open this door!"

Without replying, he stepped back to the edge of the porch. One of the other two men had gone to retrieve three shotguns, which they divided up among themselves. Each of them now stood as sentries around the perimeter of the house, facing it, shotguns at the ready.

Harper couldn't believe what she was seeing. This nightmare didn't seem real. People didn't just randomly barricade other people inside a house.

"Let us out!" She lunged for the door, kicking it and beating it with her fists. "Let us out!"

"Enough of this bullshit." Dean went to the living room. He returned a moment later with one of his golf clubs. "Stand back, Harper!"

She jumped out of the way as Dean pulled back on the club, set to hit the window beside the door, and she assumed to then confront Mr. Guster.

Before he could swing the club, Mr. Guster swung the barrel of the shotgun to the window and chambered a shell.

"Don't do it, son. I don't want to have to shoot you, but I will. This has to happen. I'm sorry."

Dean froze in mid-swing. He was unable to determine if the man was bluffing.

Seeming to read his thoughts, Mr. Guster added, "I ain't bluffing. This is important and must happen. For the good of us all."

The two men with him repeated the phrase, "For the good of us all."

She was about to ask what that meant, though her mind was racing with panic and confusion, so she wasn't sure where to start or what to even do next. Dean was still stuck in mid-swing, also unable to decide his next step.

The wall nearest her made a noise, which made her jump. It made the noise again, a sharp clicking sound. Unable to turn away from it, she waited to hear the sound again. When it did, she then realized it wasn't the wall making the sound, it was something inside the wall.

Then there was another click. Followed by another. And another. Until soon the entire wall was alive with clicking.

She raised her hands to her ears as the sound grew louder and louder. Dean lowered the club and looked to the wall, too, also grimacing with how loud it was.

She was about to ask him what that sound was when the wall erupted forward, showering the two of them with wallpaper, plaster, and debris. They ducked and turned away, but looked back as the clicking continued.

Neither could understand or speak to the madness of what they were seeing.

In the space that was the wall was a maze of writhing white and grey. It undulated and moved in odd movements of pulses and twitches as it seemed to grow in size. They were so fixed on the macabre scene that they didn't notice the three men outside lower their heads and begin chanting.

The shape paused its random undulations long enough for it to begin to take shape. When it did, Harper started screaming. Dean went pale but had enough of a mind to grab Harper by the arm to drag her up the stairs. "Go, go, go!" he shouted.

She didn't resist his movements, but she didn't help much, either. Her eyes couldn't leave this hideous shape that had erupted from their wall. She watched as something protruded from the mound. It elongated, the white and grey of it squirming as it did, till it set its point down on the floor. It was then that she saw it seemed to be a leg, and her blood turned cold.

She screamed and screamed and screamed. Dean continued trying to pull her up the stairs. His own face was a chalky-white and waxed, frozen in terror but brimming with determination, desperate to escape.

Another protrusion erupted from the mass, though this time higher and splaying the end out to four smaller points. It reached out with this new makeshift arm and grabbed at their feet as they pushed themselves up the stairs. Harper didn't cease screaming.

With a new rush of adrenaline, Dean lifted Harper under her arms and carried her screaming form up the stairs and collapsed at the landing. Looking down, he could see Mr. Guster through the window still standing at attention in the front yard, head bowed in supplication.

The thing in the wall was nearly finished extricating itself and starting to stand. Its mass took up most of the space, blocking the window. The writhing, undulating mass of white and gray seemed to be a collection of ever-moving bits and pieces that he couldn't identify.

It wasn't until the thing took what could be considered a step that Dean saw what it was made of and still couldn't believe it.

When it took the step, some of its form fell away. They were various pieces of bones, old and rotting fur, and living mice.

It was a thing made up of mice, living and dead, clicking incessantly as the bones connected with each other as it maintained its form.

As it took more steps towards them.

As it took steps up the stairs.

They were so transfixed on the horror in front of them, neither seemed capable of moving. When it reached out that makeshift arm and hand towards them, there was a stench of rot and decay in a wave that washed over them, seeming to knock them out of their stupor. Scrambling away from its reach, they both managed to stand and head down the hall. But they were stopped in their tracks by what was in front of them.

In front of the double doors leading to their room, hundreds of mice sat on their haunches, staring at them. What must have been the aluminum foil Dean had put in their holes was now a gleaming, metallic pile set against the wall.

The stairs groaned under the weight of the thing behind them, an urgent reminder to them that they needed to move.

"Enough of this!" Dean yelled and charged forward,

prepared to kick the mice out of his way. But no sooner had he gotten within a foot of them did they all move as one to avoid the kick and then swarmed in to engulf his leg. He let out a guttural scream as they ascended him en masse. More mice came from the open doorways to join their fellows as Dean fell forward under their surging weight.

Harper screamed.

Dean landed, but not hard as the bodies of the mice cushioned his fall. He scrambled to break free, but they covered him so quickly from head to toe that he had no chance to swat them all away. The mass of mice surged forward, Dean in tow, down the hall towards Harper. She jumped to the side through the open bathroom doorway, dodging out of their way as they passed.

Dean reached out a hand for her, and she tried to grab it, their fingers barely making contact. She saw the terror in his eyes and could hear his muffled screams through the bodies of the mice around his face as they raced him down to the emerging shape by the stairs.

Without slowing, the mice ran forward, joining themselves with the thing and adding to it. Dean continued with them into the horror despite his desperate attempts to get free. The mass consumed him, then for a moment stood still. She watched from the doorway in dumbfounded horror as she could hear her husband's muffled screams from inside that thing. Then with a quiver and horrific squelch, the shape constricted on itself.

Dean's screaming stopped, and red splattered the hallway.

From the front porch, Mr. Guster stood still and silent. Having finished his recitation, he was now merely waiting for it to be over. The house would let him know when it was finished. He felt gutted more this time than the previous ones. He really liked this couple and didn't want them to end this way. But he also knew what would happen to his town if they didn't do this.

The house needed feeding, and they must feed it.

It was another five minutes before the lights started twinkling in and around the house. Their bulbs grew brightly, and the interior held a warm glow.

It was done. It had been fed.

Yelling, "It's time" to the other two men, they un-barricaded the doors and set about the grisly task of removing all the belongings of the young couple. He had a pang of regret hit him again when he realized their town was still going to be missing a bakery.

As they brought out the couple's belongings, a light snow started to fall.

One of the two men paused after loading the headboard into the truck.

"Going to be a nice Christmas, don't ya think?"

"Yeah," Mr. Guster said. "I believe it will be."

ABOUT THE AUTHOR
MATT BLISS

Matt Bliss is a writer living and working in Las Vegas, Nevada with his family and way too many pets. He is an avid reader who writes about almost everything, but prefers to focus on the eerie things that keep you up at night. When he is not haunting the used book section of the local thrift store, you can find him on twitter at, @MattJBliss.

ABOUT THE AUTHOR
GERRI R. GRAY

Gerri R. Gray is an American novelist, short story writer, editor and a lifelong aficionado of horror, dark humor, and all things bizarre. Her debut novel, The Amnesia Girl (a bizarre tale of two psych ward escapees), was published by HellBound Books in October 2017. Her work has appeared in many journals and anthologies. When she isn't busy writing, she can often be found rummaging through antique shops, exploring haunted houses, or traipsing through old cemeteries with her camera. She lives in upstate New York.

ABOUT THE AUTHOR
A. S. MACKENZIE

A.S. MacKenzie is an Atlanta based author who loves all things thriller, sci-fi, horror, comics, and fantasy. His work includes shorts, novellas, and an upcoming novel, along with a several ongoing serial stories through his monthly newsletter. You can find him most days on Twitter (@a_s_mackenzie) going on and on about comics, movies, music, books, and so much more. Also, he is on Instagram (@a.s.mackenzie) where he shows off his love of cooking, travel, and other bits of randomness. He lives with his wife and whatever dogs find their way there. (he/him)

It Calls From the Forest Vol 2, an anthology from Eerie River Publishing with the short, "Atchafalaya" was released in 2020. Available in ebook, paperback, and audiobook.

ABOUT THE AUTHOR
L. A. STINNETT

L. A. Stinnett was born on the west coast of the United States. L. A. is inspired by the endless sunshine to create fantastical words of science fiction and fantasy.

ABOUT THE AUTHOR
NICOLE WOLVERTON

Nicole M. Wolverton was raised in the rural hinterlands of Pennsylvania, among cornfields and creepy legends. She now resides just outside Philadelphia city limits with her husband and two cats in a creaky 100-year-old house filled with quirks and shadowy corners. She is a novelist and short story writer, as well as a marketing and communications professional. Nicole's first novel, The Trajectory of Dreams, is an adult psychological thriller released by Bitingduck Press in 2013. Her short stories and flash fiction have appeared in a variety of literary magazines and anthologies, and her essays, creative nonfiction, and academic work are also occasionally published here and there. She predominantly writes horror and thrillers.

She earned a B.A. in English from Temple University and is currently pursuing a Masters of Liberal Arts from the University of Pennsylvania. Nicole is also an assistant coach for the Power over Cancer dragon boat community in Philadelphia and Judge of Elections for her borough. She is a member of the Society for Children's Book Writers and Illustrators and the Horror Writers Association.

She is represented by Anne Tibbets, Donald Maass Literary Agency.

Aside from Nicole's preoccupation with faceless things waiting in the dark and other terrors, she is a gin enthusiast and obsessed with travel. You can read more about her adventures on her travel blog, Pretty as an Airport.